# WHEN MOTHER WAS A GIRL

*Stories She Read Then*

# When Mother Was A Girl

## STORIES SHE READ THEN

Selected by

Frances Ullmann DeArmand

Funk & Wagnalls Company, Inc.

New York

## ACKNOWLEDGMENTS

Grateful acknowledgement is made to the following authors, publishers, publications, and agents for permission to use the material indicated.

"The Right Approach," by Josephine Bentham. Copyright © 1941 by the Curtis Publishing Company. Published originally in *Ladies' Home Journal*. Reprinted by permission of Harold Ober Associates, Incorporated.

"One of Us," by Margaret Curtis McKay. Copyright © 1941 by Girl Scouts of the U.S.A. Reprinted by permission of the author and of *The American Girl*, a magazine for all girls published by the Girl Scouts of the U.S.A.

"Secret Language," by Beryl Williams. Copyright © 1947 by *Calling All Girls* Magazine, published by The Better Reading Foundation, Inc., Reprinted by permission of McIntosh and Otis, Inc.

"Holiday for Hearts," by Helen Gregutt. Copyright © 1946 by *Calling All Girls* Magazine, published by The Better Reading Foundation, Inc. Reprinted by permission of the author.

"All the Boys," by Brooke Hanlon. Copyright © 1942 by the Curtis Publishing Company. Published originally in *Ladies' Home Journal*. Reprinted by permission of Brandt & Brandt.

"Teachers Don't Cry," by Lucille Vaughan Payne. Copyright © 1946 by Lucille Vaughan Payne. Published originally in *Seventeen*. Reprinted by permission of McIntosh and Otis, Inc.

"The Widening Circle," by Beryl Epstein. Published originally under the by-line Adam Allen, a pseudonym of Mrs. Epstein (and her husband). Copyright © 1946 by *Calling All Girls* Magazine, published by The Better Reading Foundation, Inc. Reprinted by permission of McIntosh and Otis, Inc.

"When War Came," by Ann Chidester. Copyright © 1942 by Ann Chidester. Published originally in *Mademoiselle*. Reprinted by permission of McIntosh and Otis, Inc.

"Web of Dreams," by Mary Brinker Post. Copyright © 1946 by *Calling All Girls* Magazine, published by The Better Reading Foundation, Inc. Reprinted by permission of the author.

"The Dress," by Gertrude Crampton. Copyright © 1945 by *Calling All Girls* Magazine, published by The Better Reading Foundation, Inc. Reprinted by permission of the author.

iv

*The page below constitutes an extension of the copyright page.*

"Sweet Victory," by Adèle De Leeuw. Copyright © 1945 by *Calling All Girls* Magazine, published by The Better Reading Foundation, Inc. Reprinted by permission of the author.

"Love Story," by Helen Ciancimino. Copyright © 1947 by *Calling All Girls* Magazine, published by The Better Reading Foundation, Inc. Reprinted by permission of the author.

"Lady, You Started Something," by Marguerite Eyssen. Copyright © 1941 by *McCall's Magazine*. Reprinted by permission of the author.

"Prairie Song," by Edith Bishop Sherman. Copyright © 1941 by Girl Scouts of the U.S.A. Reprinted by permission of the author and *The American Girl*, a magazine for all girls published by the Girl Scouts of the U.S.A.

"Journey to Elkton," by Constance Pultz. Copyright © 1946 by Triangle Publications, Inc. Published originally in *Seventeen*. Reprinted by permission of the author.

*For Sarah Ann, Rachel, Judith Decker*
*whose teen-age world of the 1970's*
*may still be much the same*

## In Appreciation

I am particularly grateful to my colleagues at the Junior Literary Guild—Thérèse Doumenjou, Editor in Chief, Barbara A. Huff, Victoria Mayes, Rose Engle—for their reading of many possible selections for this book and for their generous and thoughtful suggestions as to the final choices. A special word of thanks, too, goes to Averill Olsson, who was particularly helpful in the first reading of many more stories than could be included.

# Contents

# Things Are What They Were

From time immemorial, young people have been interested in the kind of lives their parents led when they were the same age. Sons and daughters have been certain that, naturally, their elders can have no conception of what is important to the younger generation. How could they, when life was so different way back when Mother was a girl?

Of course times have changed, and fashions, and ways of living. But the amazing thing is how much alike are the delights and the disappointments, the dreams and the fears of the two generations—and probably of Mother's mother's and grandmother's, too, although we won't go back that far.

To be sure, television was a rarity when Mother was a teen-ager. There was not nearly so much travel by air, and besides, during the war years, she could seldom get on a plane because military and official personnel had priority. In many ways, she was not so free to go her own way as is her daughter. But basically Mother was not much different from her teen-age daughter today.

Thousands of girls in many countries have discovered in

*Anne Frank: The Diary of a Young Girl* that a girl living in a distant country and under terrible conditions actually experienced many of the same feelings that they do on entering the teen years. So in these stories that mothers of today's teen-agers read when they were young, stories that truly reflect youth in those far-off 1940's, girls today may find that what troubled or what pleased their mothers or their older cousins or their aunts was quite a bit like their own concerns and pleasures. Boys go off to the armed services as they did in 1941 and 1942. Teen-age couples run off to get married. Many girls and their fathers have difficulty finding a language both can speak and understand.

In other words, how the teen-ager of day before yesterday felt and what she did about getting along with parents and brothers and sisters and friends, about popularity and dating, about school and careers, about her own identity, and about what was going on in the larger world of her day, too, still rings a familiar bell. Whatever the reasons for anxiety, such as war or threat of war, disappointments at school or problems at home, or the causes of pleasure, such as winning a new friend, coming to a deeper understanding with a parent, sensing a new feeling about a boy—the ways of reacting to them are not so very different between generations.

Yes, in many ways girls of 1964 are like those of 1944—or earlier. And no doubt those of 1984 will resemble both, whether or not by then they worry about their men on the moon. Many of the stories Mother read in her teens might have been written today—as the readers of this book will discover.

FRANCES ULLMANN DEARMAND

# WHEN MOTHER WAS A GIRL

*Stories She Read Then*

# The Right Approach

JOSEPHINE BENTHAM

# The Right Approach

Anybody could tell that Abby Bronson was one of the important people in the high school. It was in the way she broke away from a group of admirers at the curb; it was in the way she sauntered, her skirt swinging a little, to the wide brick steps at the main entrance of the building; it was in the chorus that rose from all sides. "Hello, Abby!" they said, and "Hi, Abby!" She was an important person, all right—and this was not because her father was head of the English department. She was important in spite of that fact.

She paused, as she came to the steps, to speak to Miss Perriman about her ancient history—and even Miss Perriman, who was not a very amiable person, had to break down and smile. It would have been pretty hard for anybody to resist Abby Bronson on this, the first day of her junior year. As well try to resist a field of daffodils in the first bright and careless bloom of spring.

She turned away from Miss Perriman. Then, humming a little song under her breath, she ran up the steps—merely enjoying, in that moment, the sensation of being Abby Bronson, of Sheltonville High, Sheltonville, New York, U.S.A. It was the last moment in which she would ever enjoy that sensation in a simple and uncomplicated way. She turned left at the door and ran headlong into somebody's big, broad, and manly chest. She drew back hurriedly. She was staring at a very good-looking boy she had never seen before.

"Well!" he said. "Excuse me!"

For a moment they stood there smiling at each other as if they couldn't help it.

"It was my fault," he told her. "I mean, I ought to have looked where I was going . . . You new?"

"What?"

"I mean, are you new here?"

"Oh, no."

"Well, I am."

"I know." She reddened a little. "I mean, if you hadn't been I'd have known that you weren't. Me not being."

They both laughed at her confusion. They were leaning against the wall by this time, letting the world go past them.

"Well," he said, "this is quite a place. I'm going to like it here OK. But there's only one thing—do you know an old bird called Bronson?"

Abby looked mildly perturbed. "Well—yes," she said. "Yes, I do."

"What's he like? I'll tell you the reason I want to know: He's the guy that's going to teach me English—and English is the thing that gets me down. Well, take themes—I can't write those things. I've got to get on the right side of this old Bronson, and that's a fact."

"Yes," Abby said. "Well . . ."

He shook his head. "Because the way it was in Morristown," he went on, "I got absolutely on the wrong side of this guy I had English from. What I mean is, how do you get in right with this old Bronson? What's the angle, I mean? What's the approach you ought to have?"

It was a little embarrassing, but there was no help for it. She always had to tell people, sooner or later. "Well," she said slowly, "I don't know if I—as a matter of fact, he—I—well, he's my father."

He pulled himself up and stared at her. He had turned a dark and painful red. "Your—*what?*"

"Well," Abby said, "he's my father—that is, he just happens to be. I'm Abby Bronson."

He drew a long breath. "Gosh!" he said. "*Gosh!* I'd have to go and pull something like that. But you don't think of anybody teaching you English being somebody else's *father!*"

"No," Abby said. "Nobody does."

"You sore? You sore at what I said?"

"No. Why would I be?"

"But I called him an old bird. My gosh, your *father!*"

"That's all right," Abby said. "You just thought he was one of the faculty."

"Yes. Then it doesn't make any difference—what I said?"

"No," Abby said patiently. "Why would it?"

"I don't know. Your father!" But he smiled at her. He seemed a little relieved.

They walked down the hall, and she showed him where her father's office was.

She did not see him again that day. Sheltonville High School was such a big place that a thing like that could happen. But it didn't matter. He lived in the same world—he lived in the same town. He could easily look up her name in the telephone book. He would most likely try to call her that very night.

At dinner, Abby made sure that the door to the hall was

left open. She could not fail to hear the telephone if it should happen to ring.

"Well," Mrs. Bronson was inquiring pleasantly, "how did everything go in the school today? Was there anything exciting?"

"No," Abby said, "there wasn't anything." Then, to her own consternation, she turned a bright red.

Her father, however, was answering the question at some length. "I don't know, Eleanor," he said. "The older I get, the younger they get. Every year it's the same way. And the less they know. I tell you, the ignorance of this generation! Pope and Dryden—they'd never heard of Pope and Dryden. A whole class that had never heard of Pope and Dryden!"

Pete Bronson, aged eleven, held a soda cracker aloft, cracked it in two, and allowed the two pieces to fall into his soup.

"I never did either," he said. "I never heard of no Pope and Dryden!"

His father stared at him. "A double negative!" he said. "Eleanor . . ."

"Yes, darling—but it's smart at his age," Mrs. Bronson said soothingly. "He'll outgrow it. Are your classes going to be very large, dear?"

"Preposterous! How they expect—Oh, well!"

"A lot of new people," Abby said innocently.

There was no comment. Mr. Bronson was attacking his soup with relish.

"I was talking to one of the new boys," Abby said. "Somebody said his name was Bill—Bill Rainey, or some kind of name like that. I think you have him in one of your classes, Dad."

Mr. Bronson paused, his soup spoon in the air. "That young Rainey! I remember him, all right! He came to us with a condition in English—a nice job cut out for me! The boy's a numskull."

"Oh, no!" Abby protested. "Oh, no, Dad. Just because a person might not be so hot in English, for instance—well, that doesn't mean anything. Because look at me in chemistry."

"I prefer not to look at you in chemistry. I avert my eyes. And as for young Rainey, he knows nothing. Hopeless. Completely hopeless!"

"Well," Abby said, stammering, "I don't think you ought to decide the first day like that, Dad. Anybody could be kind of mixed up the first day, I should think. I feel awful sorry for those new people. Not knowing anybody or anything!"

She had spoken with some vehemence. She had never been in the least intimidated by her father—a kindly person, in spite of his bluster. But Abby's sister, Martha, was eying her with a glint of amusement—and Abby was on her guard.

Martha Bronson was eighteen. She was two years older than her sister Abby; but she could remember what it was like to be sixteen, and quite frequently she said so.

Martha, in one of these tender and indulgent moods, was pretty hard to take.

"Is this Bill good-looking?" she was demanding now. "Is he so *terribly* good-looking, Abby?"

Abby propped her chin on her palm. She lifted one eyebrow. "I don't know," she said. "I didn't notice him. I really didn't notice him at all. I—there's the telephone!" And she leaped excitedly from her chair.

It wasn't Bill, though. It was only Steve Kendall, wanting to know if Abby wanted to go to a Western. Abby said she did not want to go to a Western. Abby said she had so much homework to do it was absolutely a crime. Then she went back to the dining room and finished her dinner.

After that she began to wander aimlessly around the house

—within a safe distance of the next sharp peal from the hallway. But there were no more calls for Abby that night. That, she told herself, didn't mean anything. He wouldn't want to be crude about a thing like this—he wouldn't want to be in any crude hurry.

The next morning Abby put on her dark-blue pinafore dress and her blue ankle socks and her fashionably dirty saddle shoes. She tied a narrow scarlet ribbon about her hair. Then she picked up her books and her blue sports coat and dashed down the stairs.

When she got to her roll-call room she saw Bill Rainey right away. She didn't have to look for him. She saw him right away—as if there weren't a hundred people in the room, but only one person. This was a strange phenomenon—she thought about it afterward. At the moment she merely smiled at him.

When they had all filed out of the room, though, and started to mill around in the hall, Bill Rainey made no effort to come near her. Steve Kendall made the effort, and so did Loop Sayers. Abby walked down the hall pretending to be absorbed in a very amusing conversation with Loop and Steve, but all the time she was wondering, miserably, what had happened to Bill.

He couldn't have heard anything about her. He couldn't have heard that she was tied up with anybody—with Steve, for instance. She was practically famous around that high school for not getting tied up with anybody. They called her "Free-Lance Bronson," and sometimes they called her "Hard-to-Get." Anybody would have told him that. But what else could it be? He couldn't be worried about calling her father an old bird. That had all been settled at the time. It couldn't be that, then. But what could it be?

"Hey, Abby!" Steve said, grabbing her. "You're coasting right past the Spinach room."

Abby blinked at him. Then she pulled herself together. "Sí, sí!" she said. "Sí, sí, señor!"

She saw Bill Rainey a few hours later, in assembly, where everybody was waiting for Mr. Phineas A. Wheeler, the principal of the high school, to address the student body. She and Bill happened to be in a small and animated group in the back of the room. There was one thing she could see at once. Everybody was going to like Bill. That pleased Abby—and at the same time it gave her a faint and incomprehensible pang.

It soon became evident that Enid Kirby, in particular, was going to like him; and Enid Kirby had never let any obstacles stand in the way of anything she liked. She wasn't subtle, Abby thought fiercely; she wasn't at all subtle. She sounded as if she had read a book on how to influence a man. But now, of course, it had to turn out that Enid and Bill Rainey had spent a summer in the same camp in the Adirondacks. It hadn't been the same summer, but that didn't make any difference. They were both pretty excited about it.

"Say!" Bill said. "Did you know Dick Horton?"

"Did I!" cried Enid. "And Mary-Lou Evans! Did you know Mary-Lou?"

"Did I know Mary-Lou!" he said. "Say! This is a kind of coincidence."

"It certainly is!" said Enid with considerable fervor. "And look—if you want to come over sometime, I've got snapshots of that whole crowd at the camp."

"I'll do that," he said. "I sure will."

Abby pinned her eyes on Mr. Wheeler, who was just about to call for order in the assembly.

Mr. Wheeler said the things he said every year about working together and worthy objectives. He also pulled a few little jokes that everybody laughed at politely. The session was brought to a close, to everybody's great relief, with a loud and hearty rendering of the school song, the name of which was "Old Sheltonville Forever."

Teen Townsend hooked her arm in Abby's, and they started to edge their way about the crowd. "Well!" Teen said. "Don't look now—but Enid's got herself another man."

"Yes," Abby said, between her teeth, "and she can have him!"

She didn't know, right away, what it was that she felt. It was a curiously unpleasant emotion, combining the dull ache of misery with the knife edge of rage. It made her feel like crying dolefully in the corner, and at the same time it made her feel like smashing things to bits. For the first time in her life Abby Bronson knew what it was to be jealous.

It was no good trying to tell herself, as she had told her father, that Bill wasn't sure of himself. He was all too obviously sure of himself. He spoke with the air of authority peculiar to the male of his years. His gestures were assertive. He walked, moreover, as if he owned the earth—as if he were merely strolling around to look it over. It was no good trying to pretend, then, that he might be a little afraid of anybody as sought after as she was. He wouldn't be afraid of any girl in the world; he simply wasn't the type. There was no good trying to kid herself.

Then he came over to the house.

Abby had been in her bedroom, standing by the window, absently watching the rain on the dimly lighted drive. At first she had turned incurious eyes on the old jalopy that was moving slowly down the street. By the very vintage of this vehicle she could be pretty sure that its driver was one of her contemporaries; but it took her a few seconds to realize that it was Bill at the wheel, poking his head out, looking for house numbers.

Abby stood still. Then she darted over to the mirror and

banged a powder puff on her nose and pushed her fingers up through her hair. She pulled off her old brown jacket and dashed to the closet for her soft pink sweater with the little short sleeves. And—still struggling with the sweater—she dashed downstairs.

She had composed herself, however, by the time she reached the door. She greeted Bill Rainey with the proper note of polite surprise.

"Hello," she said.

"Hello, Abby."

"My," she said, "isn't it raining!"

"It sure is," he agreed. "But it's a swell night for ducks."

Abby laughed and took his coat away from him. He hadn't worn any hat. He just ran his hand over his wet hair. It seemed, now, perfectly natural that he should be in her house. She led him into the living room and waved him into a big chair. Then she herself sat down and looked at him expectantly. He seemed to be a little bit uneasy. He looked up at the ceiling and around the walls.

"This is a swell big room," he said.

"Oh, my," Abby cried, "this house has about a million rooms as big as this! It's a house that's about a million years old, I guess, and it has all these big rooms the way they used to have 'em and nobody wants any more. We absolutely couldn't sell this house if we tried."

"Well," he said, "I don't see why you'd want to."

"Oh, I don't know," said Abby. "I'd kind of like a more modern house."

They weren't exactly talking about the house. Abby knew that, but it was all right. It was the way you talked when you didn't know anybody very well.

"My goodness," she went on, "you ought to see the kitchen

we've got in this house. Just the craziest old-fashioned kitchen! It's big as a *barn!*"

He was still glancing about uncertainly. "Your father," he said. "I suppose he's around someplace?"

"Why, sure," Abby said. "He's in his study, I should think. But he can't hear us. I mean he can't hear us talking or anything. He's clear across the hall."

Bill Rainey hesitated a second. Then he fished a folded, limp-looking manuscript out of an inner coat pocket. "Well," he said, "there's this thing. It's kind of a theme I had to do that Mr. Bronson didn't like the way I had it before. He told me to do it over and bring it around tonight. So I—well, so I did."

It was the very worst moment of Abby's life. "I knew you wanted to see my father," she said, essaying a light little laugh. "I knew that, of course! The only thing is, my father wanted me to entertain anybody that—well, he was working on this book he's writing and—well, as a matter of fact, though, he *may* be finished with what he's writing and if you'll just kindly excuse me a minute . . ." She gave him a fixed, unnaturally bright smile and slipped out of the room.

A few seconds later she came back and took him to the door of the study. Then she put on her transparent red raincoat with the hood that covered her hair, and she put on her fur-trimmed galoshes, and she almost ran out of the house. She went over to see her friend Teen Townsend, who was making a batch of fudge with a Spanish grammar propped up in front of the cocoa can. She stayed at Teen's house until she was sure her father would be through with Bill Rainey.

She ignored Bill Rainey after that. She made a particular point of it. She not only ignored him; she even managed to assume a look of momentary perplexity when anybody mentioned his name. This performance must have struck anybody as a little odd—if anybody had given it any thought. The fact was, everybody in the whole high school knew who Bill Rainey was—and everybody in the whole high school was talking about Bill Rainey.

They were talking about him because he was a crack football player. It happened that Sheltonville High was soon to come to grips with its deadly rival, Vinson City. And just at this time—when Bill's presence on the team was a matter of almost vital consequence—his status in English III was likely to take him off the team entirely. This was Mr. Wheeler's way of being intelligent and logical—and no petitions or persuasions could move him in the slightest. Mr. Wheeler did not feel—as did his student body—that Bill's failings had nothing to do with his talents.

So everybody was feeling pretty upset about this situation. Abby walked into Copeland's Confectionery late one afternoon to find an informal English quiz going on over the root beers.

Enid Kirby was there. Steve Kendall and Loop Sayers and Teen Townsend were there. So were half a dozen other juniors. And they were all shooting questions at Bill.

"Listen," Enid said. "Listen, Bill! What about Milton? He's sure to ask you something about Milton."

"Well, what about him?" said Bill.

"Well, what did he write?" said Enid. "Was he a Cavalier or a Puritan? When was he born?"

"Gosh," said Bill, "I don't know exactly. But he was born somewhere around in there with Chaucer."

Teen Townsend groaned. "You're never going to pass that exam. You're never going to!"

"Sure he is," Loop said indignantly. "He's only got to learn a few dates."

Abby put in a word. She hadn't meant to say anything, but she couldn't help herself. She looked at Bill in sudden anxiety.

"And listen!" she said. "Don't forget about Pope and Dryden!"

He smiled at her. He was quite pleasant about it. "Thanks," he said. But a moment later he had turned to Enid. "Who's this Pope?" he demanded.

Abby glanced at her watch. "My!" she muttered. "I was supposed to be home by this time."

Loop Sayers swallowed hastily the last of his root beer. "Well, let me take you, Abby," he said. "I've got the old crate out front."

"Oh, don't bother," Abby said.

"It isn't any bother," Loop said hurriedly. "I was going anyway."

Steve Kendall didn't look any too pleased. Abby smiled at him. But her eyes slid right past Bill Rainey as if he were one of the fixtures of the soda fountain. Then Loop held the door for her, and followed her out to the street.

Three days later it was all over school that Bill Rainey had passed his special examination in English III. He was going to be on the football team, and poor old Vinson City wasn't going to have a chance. Mr. Phineas A. Wheeler, being in one of his more benevolent moods, had made the announcement at the morning assembly, and everybody had burst into cheers.

Abby couldn't get away from it, even in her own home. Her father was sharing in the general relief. It would have been pretty hard on him, he said, if he had been forced to give a different verdict. He would have been a social outcast, he said.

"Well," Abby said suddenly, "I think it's ridiculous. I think it's absolutely ridiculous to make all this fuss over a football game. Absolutely ridiculous!"

The several members of her family turned their heads and stared at her.

"Well!" Martha said. "What's the matter with you?"

"Nothing," Abby informed her. "I have a right to my opinion, that's all—and it's my opinion there's maybe somebody else in the world that could play football besides him!"

"I don't know," her father said. "The boy's supposed to be pretty good."

Pete put down his fork. "I want another piece of lemon pie."

His mother looked at him absently. "No, darling. There isn't any more. And you had your extra piece after school . . . Abby, I think I heard the doorbell."

Abby pushed back her chair languidly and went out of the room. She opened the door—and stared at Bill Rainey.

"Hello," he said. "You through with your dinner?"

She stood back to let him in. "Well, just about," she assured him. "But my father is having his coffee—if you don't mind waiting a minute."

He looked at her in instant alarm. "My gosh! He doesn't want to see me, does he?"

"I don't know," Abby said. "But if you want to see him . . ."

"I don't! Not," he added quickly, "that your father isn't a very swell guy and all that—but what would I want to see him for? I passed that English test. And was that a load off the old mind! Do you want to go to a movie?"

"A movie?" Abby said.

He grinned at her. "Sure. You know. They have a screen with people on it and they talk. A movie!"

Abby lifted her head. She regarded him coldly. "You can take Enid Kirby," she said. "You don't need to take me anywhere because my father—I mean, why come over here and ask *me?*"

He searched her eyes for a moment. He seemed to have lost a good deal of his assurance. "I wouldn't want to take anybody but you," he said. "I thought you knew that. After that very first day I thought you knew, Abby—I thought you knew how it was."

They were standing in the hall all this time. Abby picked up one of Pete's little caps and twirled it around on her finger.

"How *what* was?" she demanded.

"Well—look!" he said desperately. "I couldn't very well ask you for any date after I'd said those dumb things about getting in right with Mr. Bronson. I had to keep the record straight, didn't I? The way I looked at it, I had to get that English condition all worked off before I could come over here and—see what I mean?"

Abby groped her way through this maze of masculine logic. The light was shining just beyond. "I don't know," she said. "I think it's crazy."

"Well, look!" he said. "You think I liked you going for hamburgers all the time with Steve? You think I liked you going out of that ice-cream joint with Loop? You think I liked it?"

Abby felt a pleasurable little thrill of alarm. His chin was sticking out. He looked very mad.

"I don't know," she said. "I didn't think it made any difference to you, one way or the other. I just thought you wanted to play on the football team."

"Abby . . ."

"Yes."

"Well, I'm telling you something. I never fell for a girl before. I didn't want there to be any mix-up about it. Because it was important. Anyway, it was important to me. I guess it wasn't important to you. I guess I was kidding myself the whole doggone time."

Abby looked up. "No," she said. "No, you weren't."

They met each other's eyes in a moment of blissful embarrassment. Then they were smiling—as they had smiled that first day in the high school.

"Well!" he said, a trifle abruptly. "Would you go to that movie?"

"Yes, but first I'll have to tell my mother." She turned back at the dining-room door. "They'll *die!*" she said.

# One of Us

MARGARET CURTIS McKAY

# One of Us

I was out by the lily pond, that July day, throwing peanuts to Flick when Billy came running up, calling, "Daddy is home and wants a conclave!"

I jumped up at once. Flick, who is a chipmunk, vanished behind the old stump. It must be important if Daddy was home as early as this and calling a conclave before dinner.

My parents have queer ideas about many things. And one of the queerest—according to Aunt Melissa, for whom, alas, I was named—is their notion that their children should be consulted about anything that affects the family as a whole.

For instance, we had a conclave—which is what we call these consultations—before my parents decided to move from the city to where we live now in Brookside, a suburb of Washington. Mother pointed out that we would all have to get up earlier to be at school on time and that we couldn't go to so many movies. Billy, who was then only eight, was the only one who didn't want to move. The rest of us, Ralph, Frances and Louise, who are twins, and I, all thought the lovely yard with a lily pond and a tennis court more than made up for being so far from school and movies. That was two years ago, and now even Billy is glad that we came here.

Another important conclave was about Selassie, our black cat. Last year he got an infected foot. The veterinary said that Selassie must either be chloroformed at once, or have his leg amputated. The amputation would cost twenty-five dollars. Daddy said we would all have to help pay for it, which meant giving up half our allowance for eight weeks. It meant no movies and no ice-cream sodas after school. But, of course, we voted to have it done and Selassie got well. Having only three legs keeps him from catching birds. That makes us happy as well as the birds. And we pet him a lot to make it up to him, so perhaps the amputation was a blessing all around.

I know I am too long getting to the main story, but I thought I had better explain these things so you will have an idea of the Matthews household at the time of the most important conclave we ever had. Just to give a "complete picture," as Miss Arner tells us in English composition, my brother Ralph is eighteen, my twin sisters, Fran and Lou, are sixteen, I am fourteen, and Billy is ten. Truth compels me to state that I am the ugly duckling of the family, though I'm afraid I shall never turn out to be a swan. I am small and colorless alongside Fran and Lou, who are pretty and sparkling.

Now I am really coming to that all-important conclave. As I went in through the kitchen, Donie, the maid we've had for years, was putting on a clean apron. If even Donie was to be in on this, it must be important indeed.

The long and the short of it was that my parents were thinking of taking a war refugee, a fifteen-year-old English girl who had recently landed at Halifax and was already on her way to Washington. A friend of Father's had been going to take her, but his brother died suddenly and he thought he ought to help his nephews and nieces instead. So Father said he would consider taking her, but he would consult his family first.

We all shouted, "Let's take her! What fun!"

But my father raised his hand and said, "Wait, now. We must look at this proposition from every side." Then he told us that it would mean some sacrifice for each one of us. For one thing, the girl was penniless. Her parents had been killed. An aunt had got her out of England, along with her own children, who were to live in Canada with relatives. But these relatives had little money and less room. If we took the girl, we should each have to give up part of our allowance so she could have some spending money. She would have to share my bedroom. And we should have to consider her in all we did.

"Like another sister," exclaimed Billy and made a face. To Billy, sisters were not always an asset. "I wish she was a boy," he added.

It would mean more work for Donie and we couldn't afford to raise her wages. But I knew Donie would like to have another outlet in the family for the molasses cookies and apple dumplings that she so loves to make.

We had until the next day to think it over, and the next evening found us all firmly decided to take her. Mother passed us slips of paper for the voting.

"Before you write *yes* or *no*," she warned us, "each of you must be very sure. Remember, we know nothing whatever about the girl except that her name is Elizabeth Maltby, that she is fifteen years old, of good family, and hasn't a cent in the world."

I tried to think of a single reason why I wouldn't want the girl to come, and I couldn't find one. Neither could any of the others, so the conclave broke up in considerable excitement.

Ralph said, "I'll give her my new tennis racket and teach her to play tennis. That will be a lot of fun for her."

"Maybe she knows how already—maybe she can beat you," retorted Billy. Ralph made a dive at him to chastise him for such impudence; Nippy, the fox terrier, started to bark; and there was a small riot, which Mother had to quell.

Billy went off shouting, "I'll teach her mumbly-peg! I'll bet no English girl ever heard of *that* game."

Fran and Lou said they would give a party for her. I went upstairs to look over my room. I began to clean out my bureau drawers and to plan which ones I would turn over to my new roommate.

That was on Tuesday. Elizabeth was to arrive in time for dinner Thursday evening. Thursday is Donie's day off, but she insisted on staying to cook what she called a "real welcome dinner" for the newcomer.

Even Mother was excited. I could tell by the way she kept picking up, then laying aside the sweater she is knitting for the Red Cross. We all wanted to go to the station to meet Elizabeth, but Mother said, no, Father was to go alone. It would be too overpowering to be met in a public place by such a bunch of wild Indians.

The only living creature not excited in our house that afternoon was Selassie. He hobbled to his favorite chair and, after giving himself a good washing, went to sleep.

It was hot and we had on our coolest clothing. Fran and Lou looked pretty in their white sharkskin, sunback dresses. Ralph had on his best white trousers. I knew he wanted to make an impression on Elizabeth because, instead of a sport shirt, he had put on a shirt with a stiff collar and tie, his best tie. Billy never can look anything but grubby, but he had tried to comb his hair, so that only half of it stood on end instead of all of it as usual. He kept racing with Nippy across the front lawn, peering down the road to see if they were coming.

"Shall we kiss her, Mother?" asked Fran.

"I shall kiss her," put in Lou. "She's to be our sister, isn't she? Well, we should make her feel right away that we love her."

"Well, dears," said Mother, "do what seems natural at the time, but remember, everything will be strange to her. I shall have to turn her over to you children for the next two weeks or so, as I've promised to go every day to the Red Cross. I know you will try to make Elizabeth happy."

"We will, Mother. Don't worry," we all chimed in.

A sudden shout came from Billy. "Here they come now!"

The car turned into the driveway. I shut my eyes and whispered to myself, When you open your eyes, Melissa Matthews, you will see—actually see—a refugee from war-torn England. I heard the car door bang and Father's voice. "Well, children, here she is—Elizabeth Maltby!"

Into my head at that minute flashed the images of Jane Eyre and Cathy and Elizabeth Bennett and little Nell and Florence Dombey. From the time I was six years old, Mother has read to us nearly every evening. She sometimes says I am the only one of her children who has the "gleam"—whatever that is. Perhaps she means that I never find those English stories long-winded and tiresome, as Fran and Lou and Ralph often do.

I love you, Elizabeth Maltby, no matter what, I said to myself. If for no other reason, just on account of all those girls in the books. I felt sort of solemn as if I had taken an oath. Then I opened my eyes.

I saw a thin, dark girl in a black dress and black straw hat. The dress was too long and the hat was queer. She wasn't pretty and she looked white and tired. Just as Fran and Lou and Ralph were crowding about her, Nippy suddenly leaped at her. It was his joyous way of welcoming her, but it startled her. She pushed him off, and for an instant I thought she was going to burst into tears. Instead, she drew herself up and said, "How do you do," stiffly, holding out her hand.

Lou did not kiss her. Something about her forbade it. We all shook hands, feeling suddenly awkward and tongue-tied.

Mother drew her gently toward the house, saying, "You must be awfully tired. Dinner won't be ready for half an hour, so you can have a little rest."

I wanted to go up with her to my room, but Mother waved me back.

Things would go better at dinner, I thought, but they didn't. Elizabeth talked very little, and she hardly touched Donie's good fried chicken.

Billy burst out, "Don't you like it?"

She answered, "I'm not hungry."

After dinner, when Lou passed some fudge she had made, Elizabeth said, "No, thank you. I don't eat sweets."

The way she pronounced her words and the inflection she gave them sounded queer to us. For instance, *don't* sounded like *daon't*, and *no* like *nay-o*.

After dinner, the twins dragged her off to show her around the yard and I tagged along. We went past the tennis court and along the path above the brook to the deep place where the neighborhood children go swimming.

"We'll go swimming tomorrow morning," said Lou. "I'll lend you a bathing suit if you haven't one."

"Thank you," replied Elizabeth coolly, "but I don't like the water."

Fran put her arm around her. "OK, old dear, you don't have to. Say, do we have to call you Elizabeth? I like Betty as a nickname. May we call you that?"

"I think not. Only my best friends call me Betty."

It was almost as if she had slapped Fran, who took her arm from around Elizabeth's waist and began to talk to Lou

about the tennis tournament. After that we sat out by the
lily pond watching the fireflies as it grew dark, until I suggested to Elizabeth that we go to bed.

When she was ready for bed she picked up an armful of
clothing she had unpacked and said, "Where shall I put these
so the laundress will do them tomorrow?"

"Donie doesn't wash until Monday," I told her. "Tomorrow's Friday, and she will be off after breakfast. She stayed in
today because you were coming."

"Well, maybe the cook will do them for me," she answered,
not seeming to comprehend that Donie is all the cook we
have.

I stared. "The cook? But Donie's it! She is our only maid
and she does everything—except my father's shirts."

Elizabeth's mouth opened in astonishment. I hurried on,
"If we want things done betweentimes, we do them ourselves.
Fran and Lou and I always do our own underwear and stock-
ings, anyway."

She said nothing, only dropped the clothes in the middle
of the floor and got into bed. As I was already in bed, on the
studio couch—I had given her my bed—I thought she might
have turned off the light. However, I didn't say anything, but
got up and switched it off myself. I was a long time getting
to sleep that night. Just as I was dozing off, I thought I heard
a smothered sob.

It was that sound which made me get up early next morning, gather up that pile of clothes, and slip down to the basement to wash them. I hung them out to dry just as the sun
began to turn the drops of dew on the shrubbery into dia-
monds.

Elizabeth never inquired about the clothes, even when late
in the day they appeared folded in a neat pile on her dressing
table.

As we girls got dinner that evening, we tried to draw her into the fun. On Donie's day off, one of us always tries a new dish. It was my turn to act as chef this evening.

"Don't you want to help me?" I asked Elizabeth. "You could beat the eggs."

"I'll help you, of course," she replied with a kind of stiff politeness.

"Oh, never mind," I said hastily. "You'd better go out to the porch—it's cooler there."

"Very well, if you don't mind," she answered.

Well, that was that. I fought back angry tears of disappointment. How differently things were turning out from the way we had expected! And they went from bad to worse. She refused to come down to meet Fran's and Lou's friends on Saturday night. The twins were good and mad about that. They had talked about our refugee and everyone was dying to meet her. Ralph, too, had counted on showing her off to *his* friends, and she wouldn't even play tennis with him in our own yard.

Mother might have helped, if she hadn't been up to her ears in Red Cross work. As it was, we children struggled on, trying to be friendly and to get Elizabeth to do the things we did. Billy voiced our secret feelings one afternoon at the swimming pool when he said openly, "I don't like her. She is mean to Nippy and she acts as if I weren't there."

I remembered the solemn promise I had made to myself just before I saw her—to love her, no matter what, on account of the girls in England's books. And I tried my best. I gave her my bubble beads and my charm bracelet, but she never wore them. I ignored her silences and talked away, pretending she was interested. But she just walked off, leaving me to talk to the rose bushes, or the reading lamp, or whatever it was we happened to be near.

The only member of the family Elizabeth seemed not to dislike was Selassie. It was seeing her with him that made me think she did, after all, have an affectionate nature. Selassie had hobbled out to the lily pond and was sitting, gazing majestically down at the goldfish darting about among the lily pads. I was stretched out with a book behind a clump of butterfly bushes, and Elizabeth didn't know I was there. She sat down beside Selassie and caught him up in her arms.

"Nice old pussy cat," she crooned. "Nice, poor, poor black pussy!" I could hardly believe my ears or my eyes, and then and there I made up my mind to win her. I knew she would never be happy unless she learned to like us.

Already, all of us had done everything we knew to make her happy. Ralph had taken her to the movies, tried to take her to a dance, tried to get her to play tennis; Fran and Lou had had their friends in, and they had showered her with invitations to parties and badminton and what not; I had washed her stockings and underwear for her every day, and had given her my books and jewelry and tried to get her to go over to my best friend's house. (Sheila Evans is my best friend.) But she resisted every one of us. She seemed to prefer to mope about alone. The consequence was, of course, that everyone began to dislike her and to show it, too. They couldn't help it. And Elizabeth grew whiter and thinner and more and more unhappy.

One night, when she had been with us about three weeks, I woke up suddenly. I didn't know what woke me. I sat up in bed, feeling confused and frightened. The room was very still. I listened intently, wide awake now. Then I heard from downstairs the soft closing of a door.

I scrambled out of bed and crossed the room. Elizabeth's bed was empty. I ran to the window that looks out on the back yard.

It was one of those lovely, soft moonlit nights, the kind Shakespeare must have been thinking of when he wrote those lines we had to learn in school, beginning, "On such a night as this . . ." And then I saw Elizabeth glide across the yard like a ghost, and limping after her went Selassie, a small, misshapen shadow on the silvery brightness of the lawn.

I put on my slippers, grabbed my kimono, and crept downstairs. Tiptoe, I followed Elizabeth into the garden. She was huddled on the bench under the big oak. Selassie was clutched tightly against her breast and she was sobbing—long, shuddering sobs.

I stood still behind her in the shadow, not knowing what to do. I had never seen anyone cry like that before and I felt frightened.

"I can't bear it, I can't bear it," she said over and over, and I knew she had no idea I was there.

As I watched her, "scales fell from my eyes," as the fairy books say, and I saw myself in Elizabeth's place, in a foreign country among strange people. I felt the loneliness, the strangeness. Forgetting everything else, I came and sat down beside her. "Elizabeth—oh, Elizabeth, I know how you must feel," I said. Then I began to cry, too.

She gave a start. Selassie wriggled free and jumped down from her lap. I put my arms around Elizabeth and for a long time we cried together. Then, without saying a word, we got up and walked back to the house, holding hands. Before going upstairs we had some bread and milk. Still neither of us said a word, but before she got into bed she gave my hand a squeeze. She went to sleep before I did.

The next morning Elizabeth seemed so tired that Mother persuaded her to stay in bed. About the middle of the morning, I went out to my favorite seat by the lily pond. Ralph and the twins had gone on a picnic, and Billy and Nippy were off somewhere, so Selassie and I had the yard to ourselves.

The lily pond was very still under the oak trees. Even the goldfish were resting. Presently a frog leaped on a lily pad and gave a hollow *ga-lumph*. I did not move. Only part of my mind saw the frog and the pool and the trees. The rest of it was taken up with Elizabeth and the problem of making her happier. There must be some way. Flick, the chipmunk, frisked into sight from behind his stump. I had forgotten to bring peanuts and he seemed indignant. As I did not move, he grew bolder and came almost within reach of my hand. A nuthatch crept, upside down, on the trunk of a tree not three feet away.

Suddenly I saw what the trouble was. All the pieces of the puzzle I was trying to solve fell into a pattern. Of course. *Of course*. We had gone about it all wrong. In Elizabeth's loneliness, after the shock of losing her parents and leaving her own country, we must have been as terrifying to her as we were to Flick when he first came to our garden.

(Even now, when I want Flick to come out of his stump, I pay no attention to him, or if I call him I keep my distance and stay very still, tossing out the peanuts quietly and unobtrusively. It's the same way with the frogs and the birds and the squirrels.)

Then I had another idea, one that proved our way, well-meaning though it was, was all wrong. Which one of the family did Elizabeth seem to like the best—or, rather, dislike the least? Why, Selassie, the old cat. Selassie never forces himself on anyone. He keeps his distance and his dignity.

All that day I kept away from Elizabeth. She needed to sleep and to be left alone for a change. When Mother and Daddy came home, I took them out in the yard so Elizabeth couldn't hear me and there I told them my new idea.

"I believe you are right," Father exclaimed. "Tell the others when they come in and decide on a program among yourselves."

Mother patted my hand. "I think I'll let you young folks work out something alone. After all, I seem to be doing my part by keeping out of it—as I have been."

"But you'll call a conclave," I asked anxiously, "so the others will realize the importance of changing the—the treatment?"

"Yes, of course," agreed my parents.

The others were stunned at first at the idea that they could have been too friendly.

"Gosh all hemlock!" exclaimed Ralph. "What must we be —little diplomats as if it was an international question?"

"Exactly," replied Father. "That is just what it is. We assumed it would be easy—that sheer friendliness was enough— and we expected gratitude. Well, just put yourselves in the place of these youngsters deprived suddenly of everything they had always been used to, shoved into a totally strange environment. Melissa is right—we must stop overpowering the poor girl with attentions. How near could you get to Flick here, for instance, if you pummeled him with peanuts?"

"We'd better drown Nippy then," muttered Ralph darkly. "No one can keep that dog from being overfriendly."

This made us laugh and we felt better. Then we began to plan our campaign. Fran suggested that if any member of the family thought another of us was making a blunder before Elizabeth, we would exclaim, "T.M.E.H." (I mean we would say the initials out loud—they stood for *To Make Elizabeth Happy*.) Billy pointed out that when you said them fast, they sounded something like "tummy ache." We had just about decided to adopt "tummy ache" as our slogan, when Ralph said that such a word would surely arouse Elizabeth's curiosity.

So we finally decided just to rub our stomachs, as if we had a tummy ache. The program was to start immediately.

Next day Elizabeth was up and around, but I made no overtures, such as "Let's go here," or "Let's do this." I simply said "Good morning" pleasantly and went about my own affairs. The others did the same. Ralph played tennis with Bob Overton, with never a suggestion to Elizabeth to join them. Fran and Lou went off on some excursion of their own with a cheerful "See you all later." Ordinarily they would have begged Elizabeth to go along, and then acted mad when she refused.

By the end of the week the atmosphere seemed better. The sense of strain was gone. I thought Elizabeth looked happier. Often, instead of moping by herself, she would get a book and come of her own accord to the porch where some of us would be sitting. Ralph stopped leaping to his feet and offering her a chair. He began to treat her the way he does his sisters—which, if it isn't too polite, still isn't too bad. We even made Donie stop giving her an extra large glass of orange juice for breakfast. In short, we behaved as if she were one of us, instead of a guest to be petted, or a refugee to be pitied. She must have wondered about it. Sometimes I caught a puzzled look on her face.

One evening, toward the end of August, Father announced at dinner that he had an invitation from Mr. Newberry to bring his whole family on an all-day trip down the Potomac. Mr. Newberry has a forty-foot cabin cruiser, and we are always tickled to death when he asks us to take a trip with him.

"All in favor raise the right hand," went on Father.

Of course our hands shot up, all except Elizabeth's. Father noticed this and began, "Elizabeth, wouldn't you . . . ," when I started rubbing my stomach and groaning loudly.

Ralph burst out laughing. "Your youngest daughter seems to have a bad tummy ache," he said.

Daddy looked puzzled a moment, then he caught on. "Too bad," he murmured. "Hope it won't keep you home tomorrow, daughter. Raise the hands again, please," he repeated. "Everybody in the house is invited."

Suddenly I felt as if this were a test, and that it would show whether or not our new plan was working. If Elizabeth consented to go, I would know that the experiment was succeeding. But she did not raise her hand. She just sat there, a troubled frown between her dark eyebrows. It was as if she had scarcely heard Father. She stared at me, but she didn't seem to see me.

Suddenly I felt a lump in my throat. I knew I was going to burst into tears. Nothing was of any use, we had failed. There was simply no bridging the gap between her life and ours. She did not like us and she never would. I jumped up from the table so suddenly that my chair overturned, but I didn't care. I rushed upstairs, threw myself on my bed, and buried my face in my pillow.

Presently I felt a soft, jarring movement at the foot of my bed. Selassie, I thought, must have been in the room and had jumped up to be near me, in that quiet way he has. I kept right on sobbing until I had cried all the tears I had. Then I opened my eyes and raised myself on one elbow. On the foot of my bed sat, not Selassie, but Elizabeth. She had been there all the time.

I stared at her and she stared back at me, clasping and unclasping her hands. "Is the pain very bad?" she asked.

"The pain?" I repeated.

"Your stomach ache. It must be dreadful. Oh, how I wish I could help you." She came closer and timidly patted my hand.

Finally I managed to say, "I haven't any pain. I was crying because you didn't want to go with us tomorrow."

Elizabeth gave a little gasp. "But I did want to go. I waited a minute to be sure your father meant to include me—and then you got that pain. And I wouldn't think of going without you, especially if you were sick. If ever you get sick, I am going to take care of you."

I sprang up from the bed. "Glory be!" I cried. Then I began. "Why, Elizabeth . . ."

She caught my hand, interrupting me. "Won't you call me Betty?" she said, taking my hand in both her own. "Please do!"

# Secret Language

BERYL WILLIAMS

# Secret Language

"Will you put the salad on the table, Dana? And then call your father and Tim?"

"Yes, Mom." Dana took the big wooden bowl from Mrs. Hauser and moved toward the dining room. It was her favorite kind of salad, but tonight she stared down at it abstractedly as if she didn't see it at all.

If I wait until after supper, maybe I can get Dad alone, she was thinking. That would be better, in a way. But on the other hand, if I ask him in front of everybody . . .

Automatically she walked through the door out onto the side porch.

"Dad!" she called. "Tim! Supper!"

"OK. Coming." It was Tim's voice that answered. He sounded busy, and as if he hated to be interrupted.

Those two, Dana thought bleakly. Whenever they're together they have the most wonderful time. But when I'm with Dad . . .

If she just had the nerve, she told herself, she wouldn't speak to her father about the Dads' Dinner at all. Her club had never planned one before. Usually only the boys' organizations did. So maybe he wouldn't even know this one was going to take place. And yet surely somebody would tell him —lots of the men he knew had daughters among the Hi-Girls —and then he'd think it was odd Dana hadn't invited him.

But he'll hate going to it, Dana thought. And I won't have any fun, either. It isn't that Daddy's not wonderful. It's just . . .

She didn't seem to be able to finish any of her thoughts tonight.

Watching her father and her brother coming toward the house from their workshop in the garage, she tried not to be envious. It was perfectly natural that Daddy should like Tim best, of course. Perfectly natural. Most fathers felt that way about their sons, probably. And after all, she was closer to Mother than Tim was, in lots of ways.

When the Hauser family went somewhere in the car, for example, they always paired off the same way—Dad and Tim in front, Dana and her mother on the back seat. And it was fine that way. Mrs. Hauser and Dana always had things to talk about—school and clothes and—well, clothes, mostly. Dana liked to try to design them, and her mother was interested, too. So that was all right.

But it would be marvelous if, just once, she could feel that same sense of closeness with her father. If, when something like a Dads' Dinner came along, she were eager to have him with her and knew he was just as eager to go.

She supposed it was her own fault. She couldn't talk about carpentry and fishing, the things Dad and Tim talked about. Why, they almost sounded as if they had a secret language that nobody else knew. Even when Dana had tried to read books on the subjects, and then quoted stuff she'd read, it just sounded silly somehow.

He must think I'm stupid, she thought dismally. Oh, dear,

why did the gang ever decide to have that old dinner anyway?

Her cheeks were a little pink from nervousness when the family sat down at the table a few minutes later.

"But Dad, why not make them ten inches, as long as we have the lumber?" Tim was saying, evidently carrying on an argument begun earlier. His eyes were bright and his brown hair was stubbornly upright.

"Because they'd stick out too far. Your mother would bump her head on them when she was standing in front of the refrigerator."

"Yes, but Dad, look how much more they'd hold. And Mom would get used to them. Wouldn't you?" He gave his mother a quick glance and then turned back. "Then we could take the narrower boards and knock together that little cabinet we need in the shop."

"But the wider stuff will be better for that."

"Oh, all right. Have it you own way." Tim grinned in his defeat, and turned his attention to his food.

Dana tried to imagine herself saying that to her father, but it was impossible. If she spoke to Dad in that tone of voice, it would sound impudent and rude. Tim and Dad could say almost anything to each other, because they were such good friends.

Suddenly Dana became aware that the table was silent. The pause seemed made especially for her. And in the same instant she had the sudden wonderful thought that if she and her father *did* go to the dinner together, it might be the beginning of a new relationship between them. In some miraculous way they might have such a good time that they would decide to do lots of things together in the future.

She took a quick breath. "Dad," she began.

"Say, Tim . . ." Mr. Hauser's words coincided exactly with her own. Both of them stopped.

"Sorry, Dana," he said. "Go ahead."

"Oh, no, Dad. You finish."

They smiled at each other, a rather tentative smile. Like well-bred strangers, Dana thought.

Then after a moment Mr. Hauser went on. "Well, I was just going to ask you, Tim," he turned toward his son, "when you thought would be a good weekend for that camping trip. How about the one after next?"

"Terrific!" Tim's face lit up. "The sooner the better. And say—let's try out that new patented kindling stuff, shall we? It wouldn't be much trouble to carry along."

"All right. Remind me to get some. We'd better make up a list of the stuff we want to take this time."

"I'll say we'd better." Tim laughed. "Remember the time we went off without any matches at all—and we both spent a couple of hours rubbing dampish sticks together before we could eat?"

They laughed together in mutual recollection, and Mrs. Hauser laughed with them affectionately.

Only Dana was silent.

"Would you—would you be leaving Friday night?" she finally asked quietly.

Friday night was the Dads' Dinner.

For one long moment her father looked up and met her eyes, as if he were trying to figure something out. And then, when Dana had glanced awkwardly down at her plate again, he said slowly, "Why, yes, I guess so. Unless . . ."

"Oh-oh! Wait a minute." Tim dived into his pocket and came up with a small notebook he always carried. It had all sorts of tables and charts in it—he and his father were always settling arguments by its authority—but it contained a calendar, too. That was what he consulted now.

"OK," he announced shortly. "Our Father and Son Dinner

—you know, the club's, Dad—is Thursday night. So we can get to that and still leave Friday."

"So you're taking me, are you?"

"I thought I might as well. After all, you're the only father I've got." Tim tossed it off with elaborately feigned boredom.

Mr. Hauser grinned at him, and then turned to Dana.

"Now it's your turn," he reminded her. "What was it you were going to say when I so rudely interrupted you?"

Dana pretended to be too engrossed serving herself seconds on beans to look up. "Nothing," she murmured. "I mean— nothing."

"You've forgotten? Oh, I'm sorry, Dana. I should have let you have the floor first."

"It wasn't anything important," Dana said.

Because of course she couldn't ask him now.

Dad had apparently heard about her own club's dinner, and had arranged the weekend on purpose. So that was that. He probably thought it would be kinder than letting her invite him, and then refusing.

Dana ate with small bites, so it would be easier to swallow.

There were a good many awkward moments to live through during the next two weeks. All the club members except Dana seemed to be going to the dinner, and they kept talking about it all the time.

Dana explained that her father would be out of town that night. She didn't lie about it, but she hoped they'd think it would be on a business trip. If they knew the circumstances, and that she hadn't even invited him—well, it would seem strange. Most girls, she supposed, would have asked their fathers anyway—would have expected them to cancel any-thing that stood in the way of acceptance.

And Mr. Hauser would have done that, too, Dana was sure,

if she'd asked him to. But if he didn't *want* to come, she certainly . . .

On the Thursday evening of Tim's club dinner, Dana sat at home with her mother and they made over a skirt. Dana had had an inspiration some time ago about how to remodel her old plaid number into something really super. And as they sat working together she tried to recapture her first excitement in the idea.

But her mind kept wandering. The dinner committee was having its final meeting at Lois' that night, preparing the place cards.

"We can get the waistband out of this piece, Dana. What luck!" her mother said happily. "This was a good idea—a really clever one, darling."

Dana smiled back at her.

"You're getting to be my favorite designer," Mrs. Hauser went on. She handed Dana the scissors at the exact moment Dana needed them. "I think I'll ask you to help me remodel that blue crepe of mine. I'd about decided it was hopeless, but I wouldn't be surprised if you could do something with it."

"I'd love to try."

Their eyes met understandingly. But Dana had to look away after a moment because she found herself wishing that it could be like this with Dad sometimes, too, and she was very much afraid that her misery showed.

"Now let me see . . ." She tried desperately to concentrate on the material in her hands.

Dana was in bed when Tim and her father got home that night. And she was in bed the next morning when Tim, whooping noisily some nonsense about camping in the wildwood, tore down the hall, caught his foot in the rug, and fell with a great clatter and a howl of pain. All the Hausers gathered around him an instant later.

Tim was making a horrible face and muttering something about his ankle. And when he tried to stand he found he couldn't put any weight on it at all. Half an hour later the doctor examined him, diagnosed a bad sprain, and ordered him to bed for several days.

The camping trip, of course, was off. Tim was so furious about that that he could, he said, scarcely feel the pain at all.

"Never mind, old man," his father told him. "We'll go the first weekend you're all right." He was sitting on the edge of the bed and his hand was closed around Tim's arm. "I'll bring the drawing board up here, and you can get started on the plans for that cabinet."

"Oh, swell." Tim brightened immediately.

Dana, who had come for the breakfast tray, left without speaking. They looked so close, those two, that she hated to interrupt.

But a few minutes later she offered to stay home to help with Tim rather than go to the club meeting. It wasn't really that she thought there would be so much to do—it wasn't as if Tim were ill and needed nursing—but she had suddenly felt that she couldn't face all the girls' chatter today about the dinner. And Tim offered such a good excuse to avoid it. Dana was a little ashamed of her cowardliness, but she couldn't help it.

"Nonsense, darling. Don't be an idiot," Mrs. Hauser said, hugging her.

"But really, Mother . . ."

"Now, run along."

It was just as difficult a morning as Dana had known it would be. The most difficult moment of all came just as they were getting ready to go home.

"Isn't it swell your father didn't go away after all?" Lois said. "I met him on the street at lunch hour. Listen—I'm going to fix the place cards so I sit next to him. You don't mind, do you? Your father's such a lamb."

"Yes, he is, isn't he?" Dana said. "See you later. I have to run."

She was furious at herself. Why hadn't she explained that they wouldn't be at the dinner even though her father was in town? Tomorrow Lois would ask a thousand questions.

With the excuse that she wanted to pick up some magazines for Tim, she got out of walking home with anyone. And she spent a busy afternoon doing errands for her mother, and running up and down stairs in answer to Tim's requests for pencils and erasers and rulers and things. Tim was enjoying his invalidism enormously. He had already made three plans for the cabinet—each one, he assured her, better than the one before.

His father came in just as he was showing them to Dana, and he started all over again, claiming the full attention of both. When Dana finally said she had to leave to help with dinner, Mr. Hauser departed with her. They walked down the broad, carpeted stairs side by side.

Dana stole a look at her father's concerned face, and wished she could say something—anything—to cheer him up. She realized she had spent most of her recent thoughts on herself.

"Tim'll be all right in a couple of days," she murmured. She wondered if maybe a sprained ankle could be more serious than she'd thought.

"Oh, sure he will." Her father put an unaccustomed arm over her shoulders. "But with the kind of fancy nursing he's getting, he'll probably want to stay up there as long as he can."

He smiled down at her, and Dana smiled back shyly. He looked less worried already, she thought. His arm was still around her, too. And suddenly Dana decided to ask him to the dinner after all. Even if he had planned the camping trip on purpose, maybe now . . .

The doorbell rang.

"I'll get it," Mr. Hauser said hastily, and hurried on down the last few stairs.

Dana turned toward the kitchen with her head high. He must have guessed what had sprung into her mind, and escaped in time. Automatically she set the table.

"Will you cut me a few chives, darling?" her mother asked.

"Yes, Mom."

Rounding the corner of the garage to reach the herb garden, Dana noticed the fat, glossy white box lying on top of the ash barrel. It would be a handy thing to keep scraps in, she thought, glad of something that could take her mind, even for a moment, from the memory of her father rushing away like that. It was a lovely box. But not empty, she realized as she picked it up. She might as well get rid of the contents now.

Her father came around the corner while she was still staring down at the corsage of tiny yellow roses nestling in tissue paper.

"Oh." He stopped quite still, staring at her. "When I saw you come out here, I was afraid you'd find it. I'm sorry, Dana."

Dana stared back at him, completely at sea. "How did it get here?"

One side of his mouth turned up in a lopsided grin. "I didn't know where else to put it," he said.

Dana's eyes widened. What was he talking about? Had she put her foot in it again?

"I know I was stupid," he went on, "but when I saw your friend Lois today, and she told me she was glad you'd be bringing me to your club's dinner tonight—well, I thought you'd changed your mind about inviting me. And I thought you'd like some flowers to wear. But of course when I got home and you didn't mention it, I knew I'd made a mistake. And then the shop delivered before I could cancel the order."

Dana went on staring at him because she couldn't think what else to do. Daddy had sent her a corsage!

"It's all right." He laughed a little. "You mustn't look so stricken, honey. I know I can't talk your language—all that stuff about ruffles and crepe and gores. I tried to pick it up, but every time I used one of my new words out loud I got it wrong. So I can understand I'd be kind of a burden to you for a whole evening. Probably wouldn't be much of anything we could talk about."

"But—you planned the camping trip," Dana finally managed.

"Well, that was just kind of a smoke screen. So you'd know you didn't have to ask me if you didn't want to. For a minute there, when you wanted to know if we'd be leaving Friday night, I . . ."

When Dana threw her arms around him she was careful to hold tightly to the box so she didn't drop it.

"Oh, Daddy," she whispered.

He held her. "Now, now," he said. "It's nothing to cry about. The world's full of people who can't understand each other—even when they want to."

"It's still Friday night," she said after a minute into his shoulder. "I mean—the dinner doesn't begin until six-thirty. And—" she drew away a little, so she could look up at him— "and we could talk to each other by sign language, maybe."

They were holding hands as they went into the house. It was her father who said, "You'll have to handle your patient alone tonight, Mrs. Hauser. Dana and I are stepping out. Got to see if we can't find some kind of Esperanto for fathers and daughters."

"Some kind of what, dear?"

"Nothing, Mummy." Dana hugged her with her free arm. "It's just kind of a joke between Daddy and me."

He winked at her then, and Dana winked back at him gaily.

# Holiday for Hearts

HELEN GREGUTT

# Holiday for Hearts

"Who snagged Superman Jones for the dance?" Stephie Hunt shouted to be heard over the gym showers.

"Not me. I had to settle for Benjie. And he practices drop kicks on the dance floor!"

Ginny Post's plaintive answer brought a grin to Stephie's face and she poked her head mischievously in the shower stall from which Ginny's voice had emerged.

"Want some ankle guards?" Stephie volunteered, retreating hastily as a scoop of cold water caught her.

"At least Ginny has a date." Sue Jensen emerged from another stall, shaking out sandy-colored curls that clung moistly to her head.

The stream of shower water was abruptly cut off and Ginny's drenched face appeared through the curtain. "Susie! No date?" Consternation was in her voice.

Sue nodded glumly and turned dejectedly toward the locker room.

"There's still plenty of time to be asked, Sue," Stephie consoled.

"It's easy for you to talk, Steph. If I were lucky enough to be Ralph Meehan's steady, I'd . . ." Sue's words trailed off in a sigh.

A little smile curled Stephie's lips as she stepped quickly into her shorts. "He *is* nice," she murmured.

"Wipe the canary feathers off your mouth, Stephie." Ginny, towel wrapped squaw style about her, spoke dryly.

"I only said Ralph was nice." Stephie looked up in surprise.

"Are you telling us? Class president. Yearbook editor. Head of Student Council. Basketball star . . ."

"Don't forget his beautiful soul," Stephie interrupted Ginny with mock seriousness.

Sue rocked herself gently on the long bench that ran between the green gym lockers. "All of which still doesn't get me a date," she muttered.

Stephie could tell by the way Sue worried a curl that the dance mattered to her terribly. "Well, you still haven't answered my question about Superman," she persisted.

"He hasn't asked anyone, unless he's dragging out-of-town talent." The curl hung limply over Sue's sad blue eyes.

"Why don't you work on him?" Stephie said it the way you'd suggest getting a slice of bread and peanut butter. Ginny whirled, sparks in her eyes.

"How recently have you tried to get a date with anyone like Superman?" she demanded.

Stephie stood still, arms awkwardly suspended in the air as she struggled into a jersey. Why, there had always been Ralph, living next door—an inseparable companion. Ginny knew that.

Sue grinned up at Stephie in the way that transformed her plain little face and made her lovable. "Superman is not only the new boy in town, Steph," she explained patiently. "He's good-looking and oomphey and the wolf pack is after him— full force." She swung her thin legs to the ground and stood up. "That kind of game takes real bait, like Joyce Saxony, for instance."

"You're worth six Joyce Saxonys . . ." Stephie began loyally.

Sue knotted cardigan sleeves around her neck and started for the door. "Sure," she agreed. "Only it doesn't show."

Stephie glanced quickly at herself in the mirror behind the locker door. Brown hair. Brown eyes. Tanned skin. Chin too pointed. Not much nose to speak of. She shut the locker door, clicking the combination firmly. Ralph was satisfied with her. She ran out to the corridor where Sue and Ginny were waiting. They were talking to a tall boy who could have modeled for a statue of a Greek discus thrower. Ginny's voice had reached the falsetto pitch it achieved whenever boys were present, and Sue's face just looked plain because self-consciousness had wiped away all the lively expression.

"Hi, Superman," Stephie greeted the boy mischievously, ignoring the shocked expression on Sue's face. "Didn't you know that was your nickname?" she continued innocently, as his face registered surprise. "Well, frankly, John Jones doesn't do justice to such packaged male beauty, so we made it Superman."

Superman grinned appreciatively at Stephie's easy teasing manner. "How about a soda at Mile's?" he suggested.

Stephie shook her head firmly. "I have a story to write for the *Clarion*."

"Movie tonight?" Superman persisted.

"Committee meeting for the dance." Stephie's dimple twinkled disarmingly as she linked arms with Ginny and Sue and headed for the door. "See you around," she called back casually. "Easy catch," she leaned over and whispered encouragingly into Sue's ears.

The dangerous sparkle reappeared in Ginny's eyes. "Easy catch when you've already caught your trolley car."

A horn honked wildly as an ageless coupé pushed up to the curb.

"Steph! Hurry up!" Ralph struggled with the car door and Steph mumbled a good-by to the other girls as she ran toward the curb and climbed into the seat next to Ralph, whose hair was rumpled the way it usually was just before the *Clarion* went to press, or the team needed a basket to win.

"Steph! What news! You'll never believe. I . . ." Ralph sputtered with excitement.

"Hey, begin at the beginning." Stephie laughed.

"We're going to move!"

Like a bomb he tossed the phrase at Stephie, and sat back to wait for the effect. It was as though she held the bomb before she realized it was alive and might explode in her hands.

"What—what do you mean—move?" she stammered at last.

"Me. Us. I mean the family. We're moving to the city. Isn't it terrific?" Ralph waited for her to chime in enthusiastically, just as she always did. Stephie forced a smile and words that she tried to make bright and interested.

"Where? When? How come? It's wonderful, of course. Tell me more."

But all the while he talked, she could feel the numbness engulfing her. Ralph was glad to be leaving town! Ralph was going away. No more next-door neighbor. No more steady date. And he was delighted! She was grateful that driving forced him to keep his eyes on the road.

". . . So Dad's being transferred pronto to the city branch and, holy cow, I can't wait to go!"

"Won't you feel strange?" Stephie questioned. "I mean, away from all the gang and stuff here."

"Oh my gosh, that's the best part. Everything will be new and I'll have to work. This town is too easy pickings."

He wasn't boasting, Stephie realized. For Ralph, the town *was* easy pickings and the new town would be too, because Ralph was—well, Ralph. The boy to put pep into a school paper, spirit into a school team, power into a student organization.

For the first time in all the years they had been inseparables, Stephie was glad when he dropped her at her door. "See you at the committee meeting," she said.

"Would you like a cup of chocolate, Steph?" Mrs. Hunt called from the kitchen.

But Stephie was half way up the stairs, mumbling something about a story. But the typewriter refused to produce the proper words. Instead the words that jumbled in Stephie's mind were Ginny's crack about the trolley car and Sue's about being a "steady."

"Well, I swallowed my canary, all right, Ginny," Steph found herself saying aloud. "I suppose you can't have your canary and eat it, either!"

Fiercely, she concentrated on the story that had to be handed in to Ralph that night at the committee meeting.

"Stephie, dinner's ready." Her mother's voice sounded insistent, as though she had called several times. Wearily, Steph pulled out the typewritten sheet and flung it on the table. Ralph will fix it for me, she reflected, washing her hands and running a comb hastily through her hair. Ralph had a trick of cutting out a sentence, adding a pointed phrase, and a story came to life.

But what will you do when Ralph is gone? The thought came unbidden as she ran downstairs, and it kept nagging her through dinner and later when she was drying the dishes.

When, at last, she slipped out the back door and through

the hedge that separated her own house from the Meehans', gloom possessed her. The committee members were already gathered in the Meehans' rumpus room and Stephie sensed at once from the current of excitement that Ralph had told them the news.

"What will the *Clarion* do when you're gone?" Bix Martin was saying, his eyes owl-like in seriousness.

"Never mind the *Clarion*. What will Stephie do?" It was Ginny's voice. Resentment flooded Stephie. She wanted to strike out at Ginny with words—with anything. Ralph's voice, half joking and a little embarrassed, interrupted.

"Listen, John Jones is Superman. Not me. Let's get on with our business."

Watching him as he proceeded briskly with details for the dance, Stephie wondered how he could continue to be so interested in a dance he might not even attend. The thought brought her up sharply. No Ralph. No date. She was in the same boat with Sue Jensen! And there really wasn't much time at all.

There wasn't much time before Ralph would be going, either. Stephie didn't need Ginny's reminder of it the next day as they waited for a Student Council meeting to start.

"Ralph leaves soon. What will you do?"

Stephie shrugged. "Just what I've been doing, of course."

Ginny's eyes were questioning. "But Ralph won't be here."

"Don't you think I'm able to get by on my own?" Stephie flared.

Ginny shook her head. "You do get breaks because you're Ralph's girl and you sidestep competing because you have a steady."

"Hi! Where have you been hiding?" Superman Jones came toward them, his smile directed at Stephie. Anger subsided in her, as an idea nudged at her. She turned quickly to Superman, smiling brightly, talking quickly. Ginny's eyes on her held an odd look, and Superman's interested expression faded to wariness. Stephie forced words, accompanied by nervous laughter.

"I'm late for practice," Superman backed away, as though intent on escape. "See you around." Nothing about a soda or a movie or . . . Stephie was conscious of Ginny's hand on her arm, of Ginny's voice, almost gentle. "See what I mean? It's not such easy pickings when you're just another girl competing. Come on, let's go to the meeting."

As they stepped into the council room, Stephie searched for Ralph. He was opening the meeting, speaking slowly— almost heavily. The frown that brought his brows together seemed molded there and he didn't joke as usual. Something's wrong, Stephie thought, impatient for the meeting to be over. When he walked out abruptly at the end of the meeting, Stephie was sure. She ran to catch up with him.

"Ralph! What happened?" Out of breath, she fell in step beside him.

Ralph's grin was rueful. "We're not moving. The firm decided Dad's needed here."

Suddenly the day was golden, the leaves on the trees crimson, the air exhilarating, so that Stephie wanted to dance and sing, toss her books high, hug Ralph. But he strode silently, his face glum. You'd think we were poison, Stephie thought, piqued again at the realization that he wanted to leave. The droop of his mouth filled her with contrition almost immediately, and she began to chatter away in an attempt to cheer him.

"Well, anyway, we can go to the dance together." Ralph's grin was genuine again.

"Ralph, let's not!" As soon as the words were out, Stephie wished them back. In consternation, she waited for Ralph to be surprised or hurt, but he just studied her in silence, as though he were turning the idea over in his mind.

"I mean," she rushed on, "maybe that's why you're getting bored here. We take each other for granted and it makes life monotonous." Anxiously, she watched his expression. Surely now he would contradict her—deny what she was saying.

"Maybe you've got something." Ralph spoke slowly. "Why, I'm so used to you, I'm not sure I'd know how to date another girl."

"Mother thinks we're really too young to be such a steady team. She says we ought to play the field more until we're older." Stephie recited all the sensible, reasonable words, but she felt like a phonograph record.

"OK, it's a deal!" Ralph shook her hand firmly. "We'll still have dates though, won't we?"

"Well, you'll have to take your chances with the rest." Stephie produced an impish smile from memory before she turned into the house and ran up the stairs to reach her room before tears came.

It was one thing, Stephie discovered, to say sensible words, but quite another to *feel* they were right. Sure, Mother's praise was sweet, but the day Stephie saw Ralph with Joyce Saxony hurt more than the gloating of the girls over the broken team of Ralph and Stephie.

"Steph, that was a swell story you did in this week's *Clarion*. It didn't sound like your others." Sue was apparently oblivious that anything had happened.

"That's because Ralph didn't help me this week," Stephie admitted.

"Your jungle idea for the dance doesn't sound like Ralph's baby either," Ginny commented approvingly.

Stephie shook her head, unable to speak, and grateful that they had reached the corner where she left them. Rapidly she headed in the opposite direction, stopping before a store window to steady herself.

Maybe I could ask Ralph to reconsider, she thought wildly. I've proved I can do things on my own.

"Say, I didn't know you were interested in hunting!" a voice boomed in her ear, and Stephie jumped. Superman Jones stood beside her, enthusiastically studying the window display of hunting equipment. Stephie hadn't noticed whether the window held groceries or live pygmies.

"I've done some hunting with Ralph," she answered mechanically.

"I didn't know girls went in for stuff like that." Superman sounded admiring.

"There are superwomen too, you know," Stephie teased.

"How about describing them to me over a soda?"

The jungle decorations at the dance, Stephie noted with satisfaction, were effective. They transformed the gym as much as the gay evening dresses and flowers transformed the girls. Sue Jensen danced by, her blue dress swirling gracefully and her small face radiant over Bix Martin's shoulder. A papier-mâché monkey leered down on Ginny and Benjie as they sipped punch.

"Did you think I was lost in the jungle?" Superman Jones offered Stephie a frosted lemonade.

"Mmm. That's a good one to dance to." Superman put down the glasses quickly.

"How about switching partners?" Stephie turned. It was Ralph with Joyce Saxony in tow!

Stephie didn't have to concentrate on following when she danced with Ralph. Their steps marched perfectly from long practice.

"Seems like old times," Ralph said softly, holding her off

a little. "Only you never dressed up that much for me," he added appraisingly. "On the other hand, I guess I never sent you flowers, either." Sheepishly he eyed her bracelet of gardenias.

They danced in silence, enjoying all the routines they had worked out together. Only when Ralph returned her to Superman did he speak again.

"Someday, I'll send you a whole bush of those," he said quietly. "And that will mean the field has been played."

With mixed emotions, Stephie watched Ralph and Joyce leave. Ralph would always be Ralph. Maybe someday they would be steadies again . . . But in the meantime . . . She turned to Superman Jones, slipped into his arms, smiling a little to herself as they danced.

# All the Boys

BROOKE HANLON

# All the Boys

"OK." Cornelia didn't open her mouth very far, letting the dogs pull her down the street in the early morning. "It's all OK by me." That was the way Decker Barclay would have said it. In her mind she usually fell back upon the expressions of her brother Michael and his chum, Gnatsie Barclay, the one she'd had the crush on for months. Michael's and Decker's words had more juice to them. "It's the grease." You could certainly feel that one on your tongue. "You tore up the turf on that one, chum." When Decker said that with flat admiration to Michael, when they'd been through a record with drums and trombone, it was—well, it was the fruit, all right.

But none of it helped this morning. She raised heavy eyes to see whether Margie Winter was in sight. She tried to pull the dogs down past the Winter house, but they had different ideas about that. They wanted to go the way they always went, through the park and around by the drugstore, and "OK," Cornelia breathed softly, immediately. "You don't have to turn back at the drugstore, either, because it's one of the last mornings." Then at the drugstore she had to stare curiously

down at Rags and Taffy. This was where they always turned
back, and they sat patiently, stubbornly.

*Like me*, she breathed, startled. *They want everything to go
the way it's always gone.* Perhaps Michael had been right, after
all. He'd said a long time ago that the dogs liked her best because she was part dog.

"If you knew what was cooking," she mourned, letting the
animals pull her back toward home. "If you knew that the
family is flying all apart for the summer . . ." The dogs
stopped to dig for something, and here in the deserted street,
three safe blocks from home, she could let her eyes look any
way they wanted to. "Scuttled." That was a Michael-and-
Decker word, too, and suddenly her underlip was trembling.
She straightened it in a panic to say thinly, "I'm thirteen.
Come on, dopes." She brushed furiously at her eyes with her
sleeve. "You'll like it in the kennel. Lots of other dogs,
and . . ." They ran, racing toward home, racing right back
into the way things were going to be this summer.

Rosalie, just turned eighteen and home from her first year
away at school, was going to visit schoolmates all summer.
She'd start in North Carolina, go on to a western ranch,
come back East with—oh, it didn't matter. All that mattered
was that Rosalie was going. "Rosalie's bookings," her father
said, chortling. "A wake of devastation from coast to coast."

Michael, at sixteen, had a job for the summer. At first his
mother had laughed and said, "Of course not," but his father
had said, "Wait a minute," looking pleased. It was engage-
ments for the senior-high dance band, and with Michael as
business manager. He and Decker were going to live in that
apartment over the Barclay garage, since the Barclays rented
their house each summer.

*What's it to me?* Cornelia asked herself grimly.

Mr. and Mrs. Wade were going on something they called a second honeymoon. It was to be a long trip, the first one in years without the children.

Hallie was going to her sister's in Georgia. Cornelia herself was to be packed off to a camp for eight weeks. In two days, counting from right now, she'd be on her way.

Rags and Taffy were to be boarded at a kennel. The cottage at the lake was to be rented for the first summer in ten years. The cottage at the lake was a hard lump in her throat. You grew up and things changed—that was all. Even your parents. They began to drool about things like second honeymoons.

With Rosalie singing all the time and trying on clothes, and with Michael thinking everything was the fruit, and Mr. and Mrs. Wade smiling into each other's eyes over heads, no one had stopped to think that only children of ten or eleven went to camps, mostly. It hadn't occurred to anyone to sit down and say, "How do you feel about renting the cottage, Cornelia?"

The way she felt about it was caught in her throat, hurrying home to breakfast. *As if I cared*, she scoffed, running. *It's only how the dogs will feel out at that kennel.*

She was late to breakfast, after all, and her father and mother were halfway through. All the familiar smells of home closed in—strawberries, bacon, biscuits. That hair tonic Dad was using now. Her mother's cologne. All of them formed in a fog about Cornelia, and the starch in Hallie's fresh apron was just a sharpness in the fog. Hallie's broad wink, as she set down Cornelia's oatmeal, said that it had been cooked separately with raisins, the way nobody else liked it. Everything fixed it that they were going away, all right.

Michael swooped into his chair, stepping over the back of it. "Everything's in the bag," he cracked, rubbing his hands. "I just fell over seven of 'em." Hallie was giving Michael the largest strawberries of all, stems on them, and heaped about a mound of sugar on a plate. "It's the fruit." Michael danced fluidly with his shoulders, giving Hallie a bland sidelong glance. Hallie giggled.

When Rosalie came in, Hallie's giggle went high and hysterical and she hurried out with her hand to her mouth. Rosalie had smoothed some sort of shining dark-saffron stuff over every exposed inch of her—and since she was in a halter and shorts, there were a lot of exposed inches. Mrs. Wade's spoon went down with a clatter and Mr. Wade made a noise that could only be called a snort. "Jeepers," Michael croaked.

Rosalie sat calmly with her pale-gold hair fluffed about the strange new face and her blue eyes staring peculiarly out of it. "For everyone's information," she said clearly, "it's sun 'n' sand make-up film. If you think I'm going anywhere looking as though I hadn't *been* anywhere . . . About the plane, Dad. May I? Please! Though Mrs. Soames says that if you really won't let me, then the housekeeper, who gets airsick . . ." Rosalie's plans went on flying through the air. Michael's plans cut in around them.

"We want to get everything settled now"—a new and shining something in Mrs. Wade's voice drew Cornelia's eyes that way—"for there may be days at a time when Dad and I are just wandering."

The youngest member of the Wade family chewed raisins frantically. *Wandering.* Her mother ought to know. She ought to know that they had to go to the cottage this year, like always. Sun streamed into the breakfast room, plans glanced and darted in it, the tide of general hilarity rose and rose. Cornelia was drowning in it. *For how did they know that they would all come back and be together here, with things the same?* Who knew that Rags or Taffy wouldn't get sick or even die in a kennel, since they'd never been in one? Something was shrinking inside Cornelia. Didn't anybody see that next summer was too long to wait for the lake cottage? Here was this summer, ready to burst into all the old fun, and all of them . . .

"How many are you having at your brawl tonight, Rosalie?" Michael asked, and, "I don't see why you didn't want the band," he added immediately.

"Band?" Rosalie knit her brows sweetly. "Oh. That you and Decker give out with sound. I'm having everyone who loves Hoppy, and who"—she flung her arms wide—"doesn't love Hoppy! Ask him. Gary Hopwood, of the U.S. Army Air Corps." She tasted it. "Perhaps he'll get to be an officer. That will be two officers on my list, including Page Ralston."

She was tasting Page Ralston now, and Cornelia stared at her. A man she barely knew, a man who at twenty-four was old enough to be her father, almost. She'd met him at a school dance and his sister had probably dragged him to that. Oh, well—Cornelia slumped suddenly—Rosalie would get to know him, all right. Trust her. Hadn't she wangled that invitation from his sister?

Talk about the farewell party for Hoppy, who at twenty was being inducted into the air force, milled about the table now. Home couldn't be the same even the last few days because, in addition to the packing, there had to be this mob scene. Nothing mattered to the family and nothing was sacred to them.

"I don't know why you took the party on." Her father looked tired, kissing her mother. He was general manager at the plant he was rushing to, and they had defense orders.

"But Hoppy's practically lived here for four years. Or hadn't you noticed?" She patted his lapel.

"Pilot officer Hoppy Hopwood." Michael was laughing

soundlessly. "Ozone operator. Giving the enemy a treatment right at Goshen's drive-in last night."

"Please may I be excused? I have to feed the dogs." Cornelia had practically escaped when her mother caught her.

"What have you been eating?" She frowned. "Don't get a stomach upset now, please, Cornelia. It's only three days."

"It's two days," Cornelia corrected, stiff-lipped. *As if I care*, she thought savagely. *Let them breeze. Let them.*

Michael and Rosalie were going into an old act, closing in on her. "She's turned green." Michael peered. "She smells." Rosalie wrinkled her nose daintily. "It's mosquito lotion, that's what. Have you noticed, Mother, that just when you think she's about to turn into a human being . . ."

They were about to find out that she'd been sleeping out in the tent with the dogs on their last nights, and Cornelia backed. "I feel all right," she said hurriedly. "I smell all right too. How can you tell when a mosquito is going to get into your bedroom?" She fled.

If you wanted to find Rosalie these past weeks you just listened. If you heard her singing, soft and low or high and wild, you knew she was home. If that sign failed, you could always listen in the vicinity of the telephone. "That drip! Oh! *Oh*—I'm helpless. *But* dementia . . ." What you heard coming from the telephone made no sense, but if you heard it Rosalie was home. Or you could look to the drive. If cars were parked there and if, according to Rosalie's bored report, they were "crawling with rats . . ."

At half past ten on this Saturday morning Rosalie was singing in her room, and Cornelia approached slowly. She paused uncertainly at the door and then edged toward a chair and sat down. There was something she had to ask Rosalie about the cost of a telegram, but she didn't know how to start. If Rosalie laughed . . . She sat looking at her warily.

Rosalie had to keep trying things on and couldn't get very far with her packing. Just now she was walking softly up and down with a filmy new evening dress in her arms. "How do you like it, my pet, my pet?" Rosalie asked, engrossed.

"It looks all right," Cornelia observed miserably. She hunched down, clasping her arms over the uncertainty that was localized in her stomach now. It was ten-thirty o'clock on the last day but one.

"So you slept out in the tent with the dogs last night." Rosalie's voice was casual, cool. "I thought you'd outgrown that."

"I try to do things for people when something awful is going to happen to them."

"Awful like what?"

"Like a kennel. Rosalie, how much would it cost . . ."

"Would you say that this looks like a man who's been here forever but is going away"—Rosalie was a dream frowning—"or like a man who's been away forever, and is coming back?"

Cornelia cleared her throat desperately.

"Take Hoppy," her sister went on dreamily. "Shall I break this out for Hoppy tonight, to give him a picture to carry away to camp, the rat—or wait! Are you old enough to know, I wonder"—for no reason Rosalie came over softly and kissed the end of Cornelia's nose—"are you old enough to know that Puff Ralston has a brother Page?"

"Oh, my good gosh!" Cornelia twisted. "Can't you talk about anything else? Of course she has a brother."

"The North Carolina Ralstons." Rosalie looked through her, and at something else. "The North Carolina Ralstons' Page. The rat to end rats, baby. One dance was enough to know. Flying since he was seventeen, and now twenty-four. Home for a week's furlough. That's next week."

"Of course." Cornelia's voice cracked. "Isn't it next week

you're going down, for heaven's sake? Can't we talk about something important, Rosalie? How much does it cost to . . ."

"Are you old enough to know, on the other hand"—Rosalie had plunged into an older dream—"that Hoppy was the first man who kissed me? The very first."

"If I'm old enough!" Cornelia groaned. "Didn't I see it? He said 'Take that, you lug.' It was three years ago. It was down at the cottage."

"I think Mother is calling you," Rosalie said gently. "No" —she picked up a fold of the new dress, dropped it—"it has to be saved for Page. Twenty-four. An officer."

"How much does it cost to send a telegram, is what I want to know."

Rosalie made a lightning change. In riding clothes, and with hands thrust into pockets, she narrowed her eyes at the mirror. "The Soames ranch covers eighteen hundred acres." Her voice came out of a trance. "That's where I go second."

"As if I didn't know." Cornelia's head was down in her hands. "I'd have to be deaf not to know where you're going second. What's the Soames brother's name?"

"It's Jordan." Rosalie looked at her thoughtfully. "H'm," she said.

"The telegram"—Cornelia folded her arms more securely over her stomach—"is seven words to New Hampshire. It's just, 'Can I bring two dogs to camp?' That's all. How much?"

"Why, cooky"—Rosalie came down to earth and looked at her for a moment—"you don't take dogs to camp. If you think you're going to be lonely or homesick you're crazy, because . . ."

"It's you that's crazy," Cornelia pointed out with dignity. "Me homesick!" Her laugh was short and ragged. "It's the dogs."

"Well, gracious." Rosalie was biting a lip at her. "If you

want to be the complete goon, just start wiring camps about dogs. That's all. Just start."

"OK." It came over Cornelia's shoulder faintly.

She bathed the dogs in the cellar, lingering over it. The second to the last, and it wasn't turning out to be much of a day. Upstairs the family raced, packing, doing things about the farewell party for Gary Hopwood. She listened to them. Now and then she told Rags and Taffy that everything would be OK—they'd see. But at such times her eyes were likely to be fixed miserably upon something that was rather far away. New Hampshire, for instance.

When Janie Bellows called up about going to the pool she said "No," without even thinking, and when Sara Bridges asked her to go over and join a knitting class at her house, she said the same thing. Everyone was staying for lunch, Sara coaxed, and then they were going to a picture.

"What's the matter, C'nelia?" Sara asked, puzzled. "Did you get punished, or something?"

"I'm just washing my dogs and I've got a lot of things to do, but I'll come," Cornelia said. She hung up hastily and ran for cover again. She ran smack into Michael and Decker Barclay, coming in with more bags.

"Hi-yah, beautiful." Decker grinned and Cornelia waited for the familiar plop in her chest, but it didn't come.

She looked sadly for a moment at the undeniable beauty of Michael's chum. His eyelashes were the same as always. There was rosy color in his tanned cheeks. He pushed his dark hair back graciously, and with something of an air. But he was still about a million miles away. "Hi," she called faintly over the intervening distance. Not even Decker—she went heavily down the stairs, pondering it—not even Decker could help.

*Good fresh beef and shaded runs.* She rubbed the dogs dry

mechanically. *Lots of other dogs whose families are all flying apart, too.*

Upstairs, delivery men took the back porch in swoops and rushes. The phone rang madly. If there could have been one day like other days, before—before Monday.

"Why are you hanging around the house on a nice morning like this?" her mother asked, when she went up. Mrs. Wade had about seven lists and she was leafing through them and looking harassed. "Rolls," she remembered despairingly. "They'll eat hundreds."

"I'm not exactly hanging around." Cornelia's voice was small. "I'm going to a knitting lesson. Mother"—she pressed closer—"it's seven o'clock Monday morning I—I start, isn't it?"

"That's right."

"The dogs—they go tomorrow night to the kennel. Michael's taking his things over to Decker's right now. Rosalie goes Monday night." Her voice was hurrying now. "You and Dad . . ."

"Perhaps we'll drop the dogs tomorrow morning."

"Tomorrow morning!"

"Yes. There's always a rush at the last minute. Now run along, dear."

Cornelia moved closer, close enough that her mother could have put an arm about her if she had thought of it. "Mother, do you think . . ." It sounded hollow and she started over. "That is, I—I suppose a honeymoon without all your children around is—is quite a lot of fun, isn't it?"

Mrs. Wade pushed her hair back and closed her eyes. "If it ever gets started," she said devoutly, "and if I'm fit for anything but the hospital, it will be heaven. Simply heaven. Hallie!" She was on her feet. She was gone.

When she got to Sara Bridges' house, Cornelia discovered

that she had on red-striped ankle socks with an orchid dress and a yellow ribbon. Not that it mattered.

Later she discovered that there was a place, after all, where one could weep unquestioned in a modern world. It was in the tenth row of the Crystal, with Sara Bridges and Dottie Mason and Harriet Newcomb all crying softly into handkerchiefs, and wiping their eyes to watch groggily the misfortunes of a heroine. Cornelia watched them for a while. Then she eased her shoulders far down in the seat and let go. Her tears came faster and faster. A muffled sob escaped in perfect safety. It coincided with a gulp of Dottie Mason's, with the thorough blowing of a nose in the row behind.

She came out of it with Sara's elbow in her ribs and Dottie's strident whisper sounding over at least ten rows. "He came back to her, C'nelia. He came back. Why don't you look at the screen once in a while, for goodness' sakes?"

She focused her eyes on a screen where figures moved blurrily. She blew her nose softly and the picture ended.

Dinnertime. The house waited for the party. The Wade house could never be said to be waiting in a hush, however. The phone shrilled on. A band that Michael wanted to hear blared on the radio. Hallie served special things again.

Bags were all pushed out of sight now. The floors shone and there were flowers everywhere—for Hoppy Hopwood. The party would be in the playroom and on the terrace; it would be everywhere, and on the last night at home but one. Mrs. Wade would be shut in her room with some of those lists and with the last of the bags. Mr. Wade would be at that meeting at the plant. There wouldn't be any place around for her to *be*, even, Cornelia reflected woefully.

She waited her chance. "Why don't we," she gulped finally, "all go on a picnic tomorrow? It's the last day." She waited, looking down.

They'd have picnic enough right at home, her mother said, sighing. Tomorrow she'd be all tied up, Rosalie reflected. "*But* tied!" Tomorrow—Michael's shoulders went back with importance—he'd be in summer quarters. "*But* tomorrow!" His falsetto squeaked at Rosalie.

Cornelia stared hard at her plate. A picnic—it might have started them to remembering things about the cottage.

You could always see a party shining in Rosalie hours before it commenced. You could see it curving her lips and hiding in points of light in her eyes. Tonight you could even hear it, for Rosalie dressed singing.

It was slightly dark on the enclosed back stairway where Cornelia sat and listened to her. She had had to sit on the back stairs as a punishment long ago, she remembered. If the punishments kept getting worse as you grew older—she cupped her chin in her hands and huddled tight again over that quivering uncertainty that was in her interior—if they were going to happen when you hadn't done anything to deserve them . . .

Even Rosalie's singing had a measure of comfort in it. It said that this was home, that Rosalie was dressing for a party, and that everything was all right. "It used to annoy me," Cornelia said moodily.

Rosalie was singing about the moon, of course, and suddenly her voice went high and wild and there were smacking sounds.

From the way Rosalie was smacking herself she must have been bare. A door opened and there was an edge in Mrs. Wade's patient voice, calling to her. The smacking stopped.

"Telegram," Hallie called importantly from downstairs. "It's for you, Miss Rosalie."

A flash of feet on the stairs, and Rosalie's voice throbbing low again. "*Oh, Sue,*" it moaned eerily, "*what are we gonna use for woo?* This will be from Puff," she called. "From Puff Ralston."

A telegram, even if it was just about meeting trains, could pull you out of the back stairway and down. Cornelia saw Rosalie tear it open in the hall. Her mother had come down, too, and they waited for Rosalie to say something but she stood on and on, very still. When she turned around stiffly you could see that Rosalie was being punished, too. It was the sort of punishment you had to turn away from; it was Rosalie's face white and her eyes wide and dark and her lips trembling.

"Dear"—there was alarm in Mrs. Wade's voice—"what is it? It's from Puff, isn't it?"

"It's from—someone." Rosalie's eyes hung upon her mother for help. "Oh, Mother"—it was a low moan in her throat— " 'Margaret' "—she held the telegram stiffly and read haltingly, like someone just learning—" 'Margaret asks me to tell you that her brother was badly burned—crash—family leaving for . . .' Mother, Mother." Rosalie went down in a crumpled heap on the stairs.

"Dear—now, dear . . ." Mrs. Wade sat beside her, her arm close about her and her voice helpless.

Cornelia stood on one foot and then on the other. She clasped her hands tightly in front of her and stood stiffly too. But nothing helped with Rosalie looking that way.

"He cut in and cut in." Rosalie's voice was squeezed and dry and unbelieving, after a long time. "We—we . . . He was getting to come home for a week. 'Badly burned'—what does it mean, Mother?" Her voice fought something and her hands pushed it sickly from in front of her. "What does it mean?"

"I—why, I . . ." Mrs. Wade drew Rosalie up and she drew Cornelia close to her and stood with an arm about each of them. "Where's Michael?" Perhaps she thought that Michael could help, and, "Don't you remember, Mother?" Cornelia had to touch her to get her attention. "There's that picnic at Oakwood Park his band is playing for."

They went slowly up the stairs then. Rosalie stood in the upper hall in her white robe, crying helplessly.

"There's the party," Mrs. Wade said at last uncertainly. "You'll have to try to pretend it didn't happen, dear. You'll have to try to make yourself believe the wire didn't come."

Rosalie's head stayed down and you could scarcely hear her voice. "I—can't."

"You can, I think," her mother pressed gently. "It's Hoppy's last night. No one must know about—about anything sad, darling. You see, don't you?"

"I—see." Rosalie said it after a long time. "I have to pretend, don't I? Yes." Her head came up slowly. "I can." She stared miserably ahead of her.

Cornelia went down three steps of the back stairs again. If only Rosalie hadn't told her all those things about Puff Ralston's brother. There was no forgetting any of them, and the house was suddenly too quiet. Rosalie dressed without a sound and, when Cornelia went to look, her mother was just sitting in her room with her hands in her lap. Hallie was being very still downstairs. No one could remember when Rosalie had cried. She'd put on the filmy new dress, after all, and she looked lovely and lost, standing in it, with her eyes washed and blue. Cornelia came close to her. "It's the fruit," she said awkwardly. "Hoppy will love it."

"Yes." Rosalie looked down at the dress as though she had never seen it before. "Hoppy—Hoppy's going away, too."

Cars began to plunge up to the house now and stop dead with a screaming of tires. Shouts volleyed from car to car and there was a lot of laughter. The party was gathering.

"Mother," Rosalie appealed.

"You can, Rosalie," Mrs. Wade encouraged. "I'm sure you can."

Rosalie went slowly down the stairs.

Cornelia didn't want to say hello to anyone. She leaned on the stair railing in the upper hall and watched for a while. Rosalie's friends and Hoppy's came in pairs and bunches, and all of them dressed—for no matter where the Saturday-night parties started, they always ended somewhere else for dancing. It was the same way with food. No matter how much Rosalie's crowd ate in homes—and they ate a lot—there always had to be a trek on to some other eating place.

It would be a long time before they blew, probably, and she leaned heavily against the railing. She had to sleep down in the tent with the dogs again. It was their last night of all and she'd just have to stay awake. She leaned farther over the rail. Would Rosalie be all right? Would she be able to laugh and dance and do all those things?

The party was gathering Rosalie in. It moved faster and faster and louder and louder, and how they could hear the radio dance band above all the other noise, Cornelia didn't know. But they heard it. Gary Hopwood swung Rosalie out into the hall and away from the rest. She could see the top of Hoppy's head, his hair shining. He was tall and he laughed all the time. They'd stopped dancing and he looked and looked at Rosalie, neither of them saying anything, Rosalie's head down.

*Oh, my good gosh.* Cornelia allowed herself a certain despairing slump against the railing, in spite of the queer way she was feeling, for you would have thought Hoppy had never seen Rosalie before. The truth was he had been in the house every waking minute since school had closed.

"Give, woman"—Hoppy's voice had a new gruffness when he spoke—"give with song."

Rosalie just looked helplessly up at him for a moment—
*Crimes*—Cornelia leaned perilously far. Rosalie was going to
cry again. But no, she laughed. She began to sing. The song
was thin and wavering at first, then it was stronger and
stronger, with some of the rest joining in, with all of them
joining at last. It was a strange gibberish sort of song in which
the party spun and was safe.

Her father, coming up the back stairs, must have waked her.
She sat up and turned her light on and it was almost eleven.
"Tired, Hal?" her mother said in the hall.

"Yes." His voice sagged. "We beat it though. By the grace
of God and with the help of Washington."

"Beat what?"

"The men were walking out Monday. I didn't tell you. I
kept hoping for some miracle that would save the trip. Well,
everything's fixed. We can go."

They didn't say anything for a while.

"Hal," her mother said then, "the Ralston boy . . ."

"I know." His voice was more tired. "I picked up a late
edition. Let's get out of this noise. We'll go for a ride."

The party would never move on. She'd never get down to
the tent. It was curious that she couldn't seem to stay on one
level of age any more, but had to lurch bewilderingly from
one to another. Now she was six, sitting up in bed and hugging
her knees, and knowing that Rags and Taffy were waiting
for her.

The last car rocketed away at length. Perhaps part of the
dull misery inside her was hunger, she decided, creeping down
the stairs in bare feet and pajamas.

Hallie was grumbling in the kitchen now, but at the sight
of Cornelia she giggled. "You li'l' old scarecrow, you," she
said, stacking food on a plate. Cornelia hunched on a high

stool, hair on end and bare toes curled around a rung. "You got not enough pajamas or you got too much girl," Hallie chuckled.

"The rest are packed." Cornelia ate and fed scraps to the dogs; and with her legs wrapped now about the legs of the stool, she felt anchored for a little while.

When a car drove into the garage it was her father and mother, and, "You'll catch it, you will," Hallie warned.

No doubt the reason her father and mother looked funny, coming into the kitchen, was that it was practically the middle of the night. They seemed tired and quiet and a little sad. She waited for the scolding, but it didn't come.

"I'll make coffee," Mrs. Wade said, trying to move briskly.

When her mother had the coffee on she went toward the stairs and her father started up. There were times when he didn't seem to want her mother to go out of the room. "Where are you going?" he said now.

"I'm just being silly. I—I want to see if Michael is in . . . Not yet," she reported, coming back.

Michael came in then and, "There you are, Michael," Mrs. Wade said lightly. But she stood close to him, her fingers moving a little on his shoulder and seeming to make sure.

Michael fell upon the food too. "The big operators." His voice sounded quenched around a sandwich. "Took in twenty-five dollars, broke an axle, had to be towed. We'll each owe sixty-eight cents." He ate grimly.

No one heard Rosalie until she was in the kitchen doorway, and she stood there so quiet that everyone looked at her. She moved to a corner away from the rest and that was different too. No one could help seeing that Rosalie now, with the party over, had begun again to cry. Cornelia stood up in alarm and Michael made a funny sound in his throat.

"Now, dear"—Mrs. Wade stood over her helplessly—"you mustn't. You just mustn't think about it. A boy you danced with . . ."

"Oh, no. Oh, no. I—I'm all mixed up. It's all the boys I ever danced with."

Michael came over and put a sandwich in her hand. "Cut it out, cut it out," he growled. Mr. Wade put his handkerchief in her other hand.

"Thank you," she told them tremulously, wiping her eyes. "Mother," she said slowly, "I must have been crazy. I don't want to run around all summer. I've been thinking all evening. What I—what I'd like to do would be go to the cottage and be with the crowd, the old crowd. Now wait—it needn't spoil your trip." Her voice hurried. "Aunt Stacie could come down there with me and—and Cornelia, if she wanted to. She's worried about her precious dogs, aren't you, Cornelia?" There was mute appeal in the glance she cast toward the stool.

Cornelia's legs unwound and she stood in a stupor. "Oh," she breathed. "Oh, Rosalie."

"Michael"—Rosalie hurried on—"is going to make himself sick living on hot dogs all summer. So why couldn't he and Decker make the cottage their headquarters too? They have that jalopy."

"Oh. Oh, please, Mother." A pair of thin arms had a strangle hold on Rosalie's neck.

"Why, say . . ." Something leaped in Michael's eyes, though he tried to keep his voice judicial. "Could do. Could do. The Barclay garage place is hot and the beds are hard."

"Let me talk, Bones." Rosalie tried to untangle Cornelia's arms. "Aunt Stacie would love it. I'll help her with everything. Mother, do say something. What's the matter with you two?"

Something was the matter with the Wade parents. They

looked and looked at each other and they couldn't seem to
find anything to say.

Mrs. Wade's head went down into her hands suddenly. If
her mother was going to cry, Cornelia thought, it was the end
of the world. But she was laughing.

"Dad and I drove down to the cottage tonight," she said,
her voice muffled. "Something pulled us down there."

"We aren't taking the trip."

"We aren't renting the cottage." They both talked at once
now.

"We didn't want to spoil anyone's summer. We . . ."

"What sort of family are we, anyway?" Mrs. Wade asked
at last helplessly. She'd been laughing so that now she had to
wipe tears from her eyes and the tears left her eyes shining.
"Dad and I talked," she said quietly. "We decided that this is
a good time to hold fast to"—Mrs. Wade could look very
proud with her head up and her eyes alight, searching for
words—"to everything we hold dear. Fast," she repeated more
firmly. "To everything. A summer to live quietly and as—as
happily as we can, like—like . . ."

"Like always," Cornelia finished. She stood still in the
middle of the floor, her eyes starry.

The dogs could sleep on the back porch, and alone, after
all. She took them out there in a trance. It was at least one
o'clock and it couldn't matter much about getting to bed in a
hurry now. It was something about the wars all around that
had changed things, probably. Something about the men at
the plant, and the boys going away. Excited planning went
on in the kitchen, and there was low laughter.

"I don't see why not tomorrow," Mrs. Wade's voice came
clear. "We're all packed."

*And Decker too.* A sudden electric shock brought Cornelia
up from between the two dogs. Decker Barclay, Michael's

chum, sixteen years old and . . . A familiar plop in her chest choked off further thought. She looked down at herself in the moonlight then. "Crimes," she said softly. "I certainly can't go around looking this way. Not *this* summer."

# Teachers Don't Cry

LUCILLE VAUGHAN PAYNE

# Teachers Don't Cry

Goby trotted eagerly upstairs to English composition class, her mane of electric red hair flying, her small pointed face alive with expectation. This was the high point of her day at school, not because she liked English composition, but because Tod Chadwick sat directly across the aisle from her. Tod was a junior and Goby was only a freshman, so the very fact that they were both in Miss O'Mear's class seemed to Goby to be the working of fate. Someday, thought Goby, with happy confidence, he'll notice me; he just can't *help* it! She had no doubt at all that she and Tod were meant for each other and that he was not only the most handsome man in the world but destined to be the greatest. Dazzled by her own daydreams of their future together, she would sit with her little pointed chin cupped in her hands and her sparkling blue eyes feasting upon Tod's shock of straight blond hair, his charmingly irregular profile, his smoothly tanned neck.

She slid into her seat, hoping it would be one of those days on which Miss O'Mear would have them write themes at their desks. When that happened Goby always scrawled out her theme in a hurry so she could have a long, uninterrupted period to look at Tod. Today he came in just before the bell rang, and Goby felt the familiar tremble of excitement at sight of his lanky figure. Of course, she thought, he's much older than I am, but we would make an awfully wonderful couple. Goby was fourteen, and she looked upon Tod's sixteen years as the perfect age for a man. She wished that she were older, so that Tod would notice her. She said once to her friend Josie, in a fit of despair, "I'm just too young for *any-thing!*"

"You're sort of cute," Josie had said, looking at her critically. "Only you do look young. You don't have any shape, much."

"It's not so bad!" said Goby indignantly.

She was very little and thin, and sometimes she told herself that it made her look romantic, but she knew that it didn't really. Her legs were straight little shafts, not filled out yet, their thinness accentuated by the ankle socks and heavy ox-fords which she wore. Goby wished passionately to be mysteri-ous and seductive. She dreamed of wearing high heels and silk stockings and something terribly sophisticated, perhaps tail-ored black with pearls, and moving regally through a cloud of exotic perfume. Ah, but Tod would notice her then!

Sometimes, if he noticed Goby at all, he would give her a friendly nod, but today he paid her no attention. He was deep in a whispered conversation with Joe Brooks, in the seat ahead of his, and Goby watched enviously as they laughed together. Then the bell rang and Miss O'Mear walked in, a little late. She looks sort of funny today, Goby thought, giving her teacher a puzzled look. She seldom paid much attention to how her teachers looked, one way or another, but she was arrested by the unusual silence which fell over the room and the queer expression on Miss O'Mear's face. To Goby Miss O'Mear seemed incredibly old. She was small, with slightly drooping shoulders, and behind her glasses her eyes were intensely brown and shy. She was all of thirty, but to her students that seemed very old indeed. Secretly they called her Sourpuss. They were a little afraid of her, and they would have been shocked to know that Miss O'Mear was mortally afraid of them. They did not know that her tense, unsmiling manner, her habit of saying little but seeming to think a great deal, were caused by her shyness and fear. They could not guess that Miss O'Mear sometimes felt she did not have the strength to face the battery of their eyes another day, to enforce the discipline which teaching demanded, holding their rebellious young minds and spirits in check while she went through the routine of subject and predicate, verb and object, for the hundredth or the thousandth time, knowing that they hated it and hated her for making them learn. But of course the students knew nothing of that, either. She was down in their books as a "tough" teacher and they would have scoffed at any other idea.

Goby was distressed by the queer tightness of Miss O'Mear's face today. It was quite colorless, and her brown eyes seemed dead and flat behind their glasses. Sometimes her mouth sagged at the corners, and then she would straighten it as though by an effort of will. Goby glanced at Tod; he was scribbling on a scrap of paper, chewing occasionally on his pencil and glancing about the room with an air of repressed mirth. Goby could not help smiling when she looked at him, but she was filled with an uneasiness which she could not explain. Her eyes were dragged again and again toward Miss O'Mear.

"Themes at your desks today," Miss O'Mear said, laying stacks of paper at the head of each row to be passed backward. She did not look at the students but laid the paper on the front desk in each row and spoke very quickly, her voice tight and strange. She went to her desk and sat down, speaking in a very even, very clear voice: "I want each of you to write at least five hundred words on how you spent your summer vacation. You will be graded on grammar as well as subject matter. You have the entire hour."

This was very queer indeed. Usually Miss O'Mear brought up some special point of grammar and went over it very thoroughly, then allowing no more than twenty minutes for the class to write short themes demonstrating the principle she had outlined. Something's funny, thought Goby. She saw her neighbors exchanging odd, significant glances. Everybody seemed to know something that she didn't know. The paper was distributed. Miss O'Mear sat at her desk, very stiff and straight, her face quite blank and colorless.

Goby chewed her pencil. Maybe this was a term paper to show how much they had learned during the entire course; she must be very careful. She wrote at the top of one sheet of paper: "How I Spent My Vacation." She saw Tod fold the slip of paper he had been writing on and pass it to Joe Brooks. Joe's ears turned pink; he ducked his head, laughing. The class settled down reluctantly to writing. For Goby it was an easy theme. She had spent two blissful weeks at the Dunes during the summer, and it was easy to write five hundred words about that. Once she looked up and saw her friend Josie hiding a smile behind one hand, then passing a note to her neighbor. It was the scrap of paper Tod had written on. Everybody's reading it, Goby thought; maybe it will come to me. It was exciting to think of getting a note from Tod, even though it really hadn't been meant for her alone.

She went back to work, watching Tod out of one corner of her eye as he labored slowly over his paper. Miss O'Mear sat unmoving. Like a blind person, Goby thought fleetingly. Somebody nudged her. She turned, her hair flaming in the sunlight which fell through the windows. Perhaps it was the movement of her too-bright head which attracted Miss O'Mear's attention. Goby took the scrap of paper from the girl behind her and glanced up automatically to see if the teacher had noticed. A shock went through her. Miss O'Mear's eyes were fastened on Goby. She still did not move; only her eyes held Goby's like brown, implacable magnets.

"Bring me the note, Goby."

A kind of gasp went up over the room. Goby looked at Miss O'Mear for a moment, filled with dread, and then she stood up with the scrap of paper still folded, unread, in her hand. "*Tear it up!*" It was Tod; Tod speaking in a frantic whisper. Goby looked at him for a frozen instant, her eyes wide and scared.

"The note, please." Miss O'Mear's voice was cold and empty.

Goby felt pulled two ways at once. Tod's imploring whisper on her right, Miss O'Mear's cold voice in front. She did not have the courage to do anything except move to the front of the room. She laid the paper on Miss O'Mear's desk and went back to her place, unhappy and frightened. Tod's head was bent over his work, as though he did not dare look up.

Miss O'Mear seemed merely to glance at the note, but in that moment her face crumpled and sagged. Then she sat up straight and stiff again, her face masklike, saying nothing at all. She did not even speak when the bell rang, and the students passed their papers up to the front without being told. They scrambled for the door even faster than usual. Goby went out slowly. By the time she reached the door the room was empty.

"Please shut the door as you leave," said Miss O'Mear.

Goby stepped out into the hall, shutting the door behind her, full of a vast relief because Miss O'Mear had not called her back to be grilled about the note. Most of the students were already at their lockers, and as Goby started for her own she realized suddenly that she had forgotten to turn in her theme. She saw Tod standing at the stairs, looking her way. Maybe he's waiting to tell me what was in that note, she thought excitedly. I didn't even get to read it. But she was afraid to leave without turning in her paper, so she went back to the classroom hurriedly and opened the door.

"I forgot to turn this in, Miss O'Mear," she began, but stopped suddenly with a little startled exclamation. "Wh— what's the matter?"

Miss O'Mear sat with her head down on her arms, her shoulders shaking. Why, she's crying! thought Goby with an awful sinking of her heart.

"Are you sick or something?" she stammered.

It was incredible and horrible that a teacher should cry. Teachers don't do that, thought Goby with dismay; not *teachers*. She felt confused and a little frightened.

Miss O'Mear raised her head and looked at Goby, not trying to wipe away the tears. She had taken off her glasses and her ravaged face looked somehow very young and defenseless.

"Teachers aren't supposed to cry, are they?" she asked in a little shaking voice. "No. They don't have any feelings. They're not even supposed to b-be human." She paid no attention at all to Goby's theme paper, as though she did not even see it. "I'm shocking you," she said. She put her hand suddenly to her eyes with hard pressure. "I don't care. I just don't care any more."

"I—I'm s-sorry," Goby stammered, standing very still and twisting her hands. She did not know what was the matter with Miss O'Mear and did not know what to do.

"Here," said Miss O'Mear in a little bitter voice, and she held out the scrap of paper which Goby had laid on her desk. "You might as well read it. I suppose everybody in the class has read it by now, and of course it's very funny; it's terribly funny. Such a joke. We ought to put it up on the main bulletin board so everybody can g-get a big laugh . . ."

Goby took the note, not knowing what else to do. She read it quickly:

> *Listen, my children, and you shall hear*
> *Screams of rage from Sourpuss O'Mear.*
> *Pity the kids in her classes today—*
> *The rope wore out and her man got away.*

"Wh—what does it mean?" she whispered.

"Oh," said Miss O'Mear. "You don't know?" She looked at Goby for a long instant. "You must be the only one who hasn't had a laugh out of it yet," she said. "I was going to stop teaching next year. I was going to be married."

"Oh," said Goby.

"That's the first part of the joke," said Miss O'Mear. "The old maid teacher has a boy friend. That's awfully funny."

Goby sat quietly and miserably, waiting.

"Now, I'm—not going to be married," said Miss O'Mear in a dead voice.

Tears came to Goby's eyes. She burst out wretchedly: "It's awful! It's a mean, awful note!"

"No," said Miss O'Mear tonelessly. "It doesn't matter. The note—it was just a—last straw. Nobody likes to be kicked in the face when he's down. Even by children." Her attempt to smile made Goby ache. "I'm sorry I let you see me like this, Goby. You're a nice child. Run along now and forget about this."

"I'm terribly sorry, Miss O'Mear," said Goby, close to tears.

"They say if you teach long enough you get a hard shell around you and the students can't hurt you any more," said Miss O'Mear, as though she had forgotten all about Goby.

"You don't mean to be cruel, you're just young." She looked up. "Please go now, Goby."

Goby went out softly. It was her lunch hour, but she didn't want to eat. She walked forlornly toward the stairs and almost bumped into Tod. He looked at her challengingly.

"I suppose you went in to tell her I wrote that note."

Goby stood looking at him, her blue eyes narrow and icy with contempt. I must remember what he looks like, she thought; I must remember a person can look like Tod and still do mean, terrible things. He shifted uncomfortably.

"She's crying," said Goby finally. "She's in there crying."

He looked at her in shocked silence.

"I used to wish you'd notice me," said Goby. "I used to think you were wonderful."

He stared at her, startled and blushing.

"Now," said Goby in a little, high, breaking voice, "I don't think I like you very much." She turned and left him, her short pleated skirt swirling as she went down the stairs very fast, almost defiantly.

After that she would not look at him in class, and if his eyes met hers she answered with a cool, unsmiling stare. After a time it seemed that nothing was left of the whole incident except that Goby no longer spent her time in class daydreaming about Tod. She was afraid that if she looked at him very much she would weaken and begin liking him again. Because he doesn't really look mean, she told herself sadly.

Sometimes she knew that Tod was trying to catch her eye, but she sat looking straight ahead with her mouth firmly set and her blue eyes unseeing. He was more subdued in class, and afterward he would lounge about awkwardly, watching her. He wants to talk to me now, he wants to be friendly, she thought scornfully. But in her mind she added unhappily, I want to be friendly, too. One day he cornered her in the hall and stood uneasily, jingling a few coins in his pocket.

"You—you got a date for Sunday night, Goby?"

"No."

"Would you like to go to the movies with me?"

It was a frightful temptation. "I—I don't think my mother would let me. I can't."

"How about Saturday?"

"I'm sorry," she lied. "I'm busy."

"Well," he said. "Gee." He craned his head about and saw Joe Brooks. "I'll see ya later," he said to Goby, and loped off to join Joe.

I *want* to go with him! mourned Goby. Why didn't I say yes? Oh, Goby, you crazy fool! He'll never ask me again, she thought despairingly. But she couldn't forget Miss O'Mear's hurt white face.

One day the office girl came to Miss O'Mear's room to tell her she was wanted on the phone. "It's long distance," she said in answer to the teacher's surprised and questioning look.

"Oh," said Miss O'Mear, her face suddenly very white. She looked distractedly about the room. "Tod, will you take over while I'm gone? Try to go on with the lesson and keep order, please." She hurried out of the room.

Tod walked up to her desk, looking a little abashed. An eager buzz started over the room and he rapped on the desk with sudden authority.

"Now look, kids," he said. "I want you to be quiet."

"Look who's talkin'!" exclaimed Joe Brooks, guffawing.

"Shut up, Joe," Tod said, frowning at his friend. "The bell's going to ring pretty soon. I want to say something and I want everybody to be quiet for a minute."

"OK, OK," somebody said, bored.

"Well," said Tod, "I guess most of you remember that day

I wrote that little poem about Miss O'Mear and she took it away from Goby." The class grew eager and intent, wondering. Tod hitched his thumbs in his belt and stared frowningly at the desk blotter. "Well," he said, "I guess Miss O'Mear felt pretty bad about it, and afterward I was ashamed because I did it. And I apologized to her. Some teachers would make it hot for you in class for a thing like that, but Miss O'Mear never did."

Goby couldn't believe it. She sat with parted lips, her eyes shining at Tod.

Tod paused and looked around the room helplessly. "I guess I just thought I was being pretty smart. I guess I just didn't even stop to think that teachers have feelings. I just want to say I'll never do anything like that again, and if any of you other guys do, I'll—" he stood looking at them belligerently, his face very pink—"I'll push your face in."

The students looked at him, startled, then at one another, and then a little wave of laughter went over the room. Suddenly everybody was laughing and clapping, and Tod, forgetting that he was supposed to be watching the class, started back for his seat. He kept his eyes straight on Goby, and she could feel him looking at her. She raised her head until her eyes met his and then she smiled.

Just at that moment Miss O'Mear walked back into the room, but she did not even seem to notice that the class was not in order. She sounded breathless.

"It's almost time for the bell," she said, "and if you leave quietly you may go right now." Overjoyed, the class tumbled toward the door. "Quietly, please!" cried Miss O'Mear, but she was smiling and there was a new quality in her voice, something strong and happy.

But Goby did not notice. She was looking at Tod, and in

both of them was a trembling consciousness that everything between them was all right.

"Goby," said Miss O'Mear.

Goby turned to look at the teacher.

"Maybe I won't be teaching next year, after all, Goby."

At first the words were meaningless. It was the only reference either of them had ever made to their conversation on the day Miss O'Mear had read the note. Then, seeing the teacher's transfigured face, remembering the long-distance phone call, understanding swept over Goby.

"Oh!" she cried. "I'm so glad!"

She went out of the room swiftly, knowing that Tod would be waiting for her, and it was quite natural and right that she should walk up to him.

"Hi," said Goby, speaking softly.

"Hi," said Tod.

Understanding lay between them sweetly and without strain as their eyes met in a long look. There was no need for questions nor for any explanations.

"Would you go skating with me tomorrow night, Goby?"

"Yes," Goby said simply.

She knew it was the beginning of a long and lovely chapter in her life.

# The Widening Circle

BERYL EPSTEIN

# The Widening Circle

Dodo Spencer spooned jam generously onto her plate and said across the breakfast table to her brother, "Pan, please."

Ed handed her the plate of bread and grinned an automatic recognition of the joke. Dodo had been quoting, as they so often did to each other, Joe Cantwell's phrase which had become a classic with the gang when they spent a weekend together at the Spencers' summer cottage the previous season. All that weekend Joe had said, "Pan, please," whenever he wanted bread. And they had laughed uproariously at his purely American pronunciation of one of the first words they had all learned in French class—until on Sunday evening he announced loftily he hadn't been trying to talk French at all. He'd been, he said, merely referring to the fact that the Spencers had been using a pie pan for a bread plate, having run out of dishes for their four young guests. But ever after that, *pan* had been the gang's word for bread—in fact, for almost any kind of food. They had lots of words like that, just as they had so many memories in common.

"Peg and Kit and I are going shopping for our May Dance dresses Saturday," Dodo went on, spreading the jam. "Any particular color you like best on Peg? You might as well say now."

"I—er . . ." Ed stopped and took a long swallow of milk and began again. "I'm not planning to ask Peg," he announced.

"You're *not?*" Dodo's voice was incredulous. "Oh—you mean you and Stevie are going to swap? That he's going to take Peg and you're going to take Kit?"

"I'm taking Martha Schmidt," Ed told her. He shoved his napkin into its ring. "May I be excused now, Mom? Dad?"

"If you're sure you had enough breakfast, dear."

"All right, son."

Ed pushed back his chair and got up.

"Ed Spencer! You come right back here!" Dodo clutched at his sweater sleeve as he went past her, and hung on hard. "Are you head-crazy?" That was another gang word; they saved *crazy* for something especially nice, but head-crazy meant loop-happy, out of time—in other words, out of one's mind.

"Not that I am aware," Ed said coldly, trying to jerk away. "But you don't have to pump up any tears for Peg. She's getting a bid. Hank Arnold confided in my shell-like ear just yesterday that he wanted to ask her, if I hadn't beaten him to it, so I said go ahead. Because I'd already made up my mind I wanted to take Mart. And now if you've finished clawing at my garment, I'd like to get on my way."

"I certainly have not finished. Please excuse me, Mother. 'Bye, Dad. See you at noon." And Dodo, still hanging onto Ed's arm, went with him out into the hall where they both picked up their books. "Of course Peg would get a bid—she and I've known for ages that Hank wanted to date her. But that's not the point! It means the gang won't be together— and for the May Dance!"

"So what?" They clattered down the front steps, side by side. "Don't you get a little tired of the gang being together all the time?"

"Of course not!" Dodo looked shocked. "Why, we practically have a pact."

"Yeah. You'd think we had, the way we ignore everybody else."

"But we *like* each other best—we figured that out long ago. So why should we bother with other people?"

"Well, I'm bothering—this time. It's not that I don't like Peg. I just feel like taking Martha, and so I'm going to. In fact, I asked her yesterday."

"Oh—you!"

For once, words failed Dodo, and before she could rally again, they had reached the corner where Dodo always waited for Peg and Kit, and where Ed left her to pick up Stevie and Joe in the middle of the next block. So she let him go, and stood leaning against a tree as she thought over the cataclysm that had just struck. Because that's what it was, definitely. What fun would the biggest dance of the season be if the gang didn't go to it together and stop together for hamburgers at the Spencers' or at Peg's afterward?

"Hi!" And there was Peg herself, in a plaid skirt like Dodo's, with her scarf tied the same way around her head and wearing her string of plastic measuring spoons, their bowls painted with caricatures of the gang's faces. The tiny heads seemed to grin at the matching heads dangling around Dodo's neck. Only the girls' sweaters were different—Peg's green to go with her auburn hair and Dodo's the bright red you can wear if your hair is really yellow.

In two minutes Dodo had told her the whole sad tale. At first Peg seemed almost more interested than upset to learn that her bid for the dance was to come from Hank.

"I'd always kind of wondered what it would be like to go out with him," she said curiously.

"But you wouldn't—not and break up the crowd," Dodo reminded her, a little annoyed that Peg didn't quite seem to realize the seriousness of the situation. "But that's just what Ed's going to do—unless we stop him."

"But how could we? If he's already asked her?"

Dodo had been thinking about that. "We could get somebody to explain it to Martha—you know, tell her she wouldn't have a good time. And she wouldn't, being an outsider, sort of. I'd do it myself, only it might be better coming from . . ."

"Don't look at *me!*"

"No. You're right. She might just think you were jealous, and not understand at all. I'll tell you—we'll get Kit to do it."

But by the time Kit had joined them (Kit's sweater was blue to match her very blue eyes), Dodo had another plan. And when they had told Kit the story, she offered it.

"You're always hearing how grownups handle these things," she began. "When a woman finds out her son is going to marry some terrible creature who simply wouldn't fit in at all, she . . ."

"Martha's not a terrible creature," Peg objected.

"I didn't say she was," Dodo said impatiently. "But you must admit she wouldn't fit in. I mean nobody would. We want to stay the way we are now. Don't we?"

"I guess you're right," Kit said.

"I suppose so," Peg murmured.

"Of course. So we'll have a little get-together—say at our house tomorrow night—and we'll tell Ed to bring Martha. And it'll work out the way it does when grownups invite the girl to dinner."

"And how's that?"

"Oh, Peg, don't be so dismally dull. In the stories, the girl realizes she doesn't belong and she breaks the engagement. And it's better for everybody that way. So maybe after to-morrow night Martha and Ed will both change their minds and everything will be pistachio." *Pistachio* was the gang's latest word for wonderful.

"I suppose it might work," Kit said.

"Of course it will. And after all," Dodo repeated, because in spite of herself she didn't feel completely comfortable about her plan, "it'll be for her own good as much as ours."

The next evening started off perfectly. For one thing, Dodo and Peg and Kit all wore slacks, and Martha arrived in a date dress. She looked pretty, and Dodo could understand per-fectly well her brother's admiration for Martha's slim black-haired style, but she certainly looked *different*.

And then there was the business of introducing her to Mr. and Mrs. Spencer. They were both friendly and tried to make her feel at home. But Dodo thought their very friendliness must make it apparent to Martha how differently they treated her than they treated the others, who had long ago been pro-moted to the casualness with which the Spencers spoke to their own daughter and son.

There was only one bad moment, really—when Dodo took Martha upstairs to leave her coat. She could tell Martha was a little nervous, because she stopped to comb her hair even though it looked perfect the way it was.

"I wish I'd worn slacks," she said then. "I guess I thought . . ." She stopped, shyly.

"Don't worry," Dodo assured her. "You look pistachio. Wonderful, I mean," she explained kindly. "Of course our gang always wears slacks when we're just hanging around at home, but it doesn't matter at all."

It did, though. They both knew that.

It was while Martha was twining a curl around her finger

that she turned slightly and said, "It was nice of you to ask me over. Maybe now that we're better acquainted you and Ed will come over to my house sometime."

"Of course," Dodo said brightly.

"In fact, I was thinking—I talked to Mother about it tonight—and we thought maybe before the dance you'd . . ."

Suddenly Dodo knew what Martha was going to suggest, and she couldn't let her. Martha was going to ask Ed and Dodo and her date to dinner before the dance. It would be awkward to refuse now, but neither could she accept when . . . Swiftly Dodo swallowed her manners and her suddenly remorseful conscience with one gulp.

"They've already got the records on," she said, grabbing Martha's hand and laughing as if she were entirely unaware that she had interrupted her. "Come on."

It sounded rude and impolite, but Dodo told herself that really she was just being cruel in order to be kind. (She'd read that phrase somewhere, she thought. In Shakespeare, maybe?) Because actually it would have been worse for Martha to have gone through with the invitation in view of what was certain to happen tonight.

A few minutes later Dodo was sure she had been right. Everything was going just as she'd known it would—and as it would go on the night of the May Dance if she didn't prevent it.

Kit and Stevie and Peg and Joe were already dancing when the two girls reached the living room and Ed took Martha's other hand and pulled her into a fast dance. Dodo let her go with a smile, and did a couple of turns by herself as if she didn't care whether she had a partner or not. She did, naturally, and it occurred to her that it might have been a good idea to have asked Hank tonight, in order to even things up. But probably it was best as it was.

And then she noticed that Martha wasn't following very well. That wasn't surprising. Ed had a lot of tricky turns and they were difficult to keep up with if you hadn't danced with him a lot. Martha's cheeks grew an embarrassed pink. When Joe and Stevie danced with Martha the same thing happened.

"You people all dance so wonderfully together," Martha said once wistfully, as she and Dodo stood side by side while Ed was changing a record.

"It would be surprising if we didn't," Dodo said casually. "After all, we spend practically all our time doing it."

When they finally stopped for a round of Cokes, Stevie said, staring at the table with simulated amazement, "What? No pan?"

The gang laughed.

"That's for later," Dodo told him. "And it'll be pistachio. Honestly. I made it myself."

Martha, smiling uncertainly in the midst of their laughter, said, "Pistachio bread? And you made it, Dodo? It sounds wonderful."

At which everybody laughed much louder than before, except Ed who got rather red and explained very carefully to Martha the source of the joke.

"Ziggedy! That was some weekend, wasn't it?" Joe picked it up.

"Was it! Remember when Peg was sitting on the end of the diving board and you ran out on it, Ed, and . . ."

But that was as far as Kit got. It was about as far as most of their memories needed to be put into words, before the gang caught on. In another instant they were all laughing again.

The stories of their good times together flew thick and fast after that, and Dodo could see that Ed was having to spend a good deal of time explaining things to Martha as they went along. He got redder and redder. Martha just smiled steadily, but above the smile her eyes grew more wistful.

They broke up a little earlier than usual, and Dodo was glad of that. On the whole, the evening had been quite a strain. But worth it, of course.

She and Martha were alone again in her bedroom at the last. Kit and Peg had shut themselves into the bathroom to repair their faces and, Dodo surmised, to compare notes on their success.

"Could I give you powder? Or anything?" Dodo asked, a little ill at ease.

"No, thanks." Martha smiled her tense smile into the mirror.

When she turned around again she seemed to be bracing herself. "I don't quite know how to say, this, Dodo," she began. "But . . ."

Dodo swallowed. It was coming. And it *would* be better. It really would—for Martha, too.

"I mean—maybe if I didn't say anything at all, you'd think it was sort of funny. But I hope you'll understand," Martha floundered on. "I wouldn't want you to think I meant to be rude."

"Of course I won't," Dodo said quickly. But she wished Martha would tell Ed instead of her.

"Well, when we were up here before, I started to ask you something, and I suppose you guessed what it was. So I'd better—I mean . . ." Martha met Dodo's eyes directly in the mirror and then rushed on, looking unhappy. "I was going to ask you and Ed and your date—it's Joe, isn't it?—to dinner on the night of the dance. But I guess maybe it would be better not to. Only please understand, Dodo, that it isn't anything —anything . . ."

"Anything personal, you mean?" Dodo suggested, trying to help her out, trying to get it finished and done with.

"That's right. It's nothing personal at all." Martha had seized gratefully on the word. "It's just that my brother will be home that week—he's been overseas, you know—and he's bringing these two other sailors with him. And they all wanted to come to the dance stag. Only, of course, Bill says they'll all feel sort of strange. That's why I thought it might be good to have some people in for dinner, so we could all go together. I *know* they'll be all right, once we get there. Bill's awfully handsome, and I've seen pictures of these other two boys and they look sharp, too. But it was just that I thought they might feel more at home, right at the beginning, if there was more than one girl around."

She took a long breath and waited a moment, as if perhaps Dodo would help her out again. But Dodo was staring at Martha's small, wretched face in the mirror and she couldn't have spoken if her life depended on it.

So finally Martha went on. "Only everybody in your crowd seems so—so sort of—I don't know what the word is, exactly. But I'm afraid it might make the boys feel even lonelier. Not wanted, sort of. Not really at home. But I'm sure you'll like my brother when you meet him. Maybe you wouldn't mind dancing with him once at the dance?"

After a rather long moment, Dodo managed to speak. "No," she said. "I wouldn't mind at all."

But inside her head, words were tumbling around dizzily.

She could have arrived at the May dance with Joe and Ed and three other men—five escorts for two girls. And three of them older men—heroes, probably. It would have been the kind of evening girls dream of. And Martha, who apparently didn't realize that coming with four men herself would make her the talk of High for months—Martha had been going to share it with her.

Only she wasn't going to now. Martha had changed her mind.

"It serves me right," Dodo said.

"What did you say, Dodo? You do understand, don't you?"

Dodo turned finally, and forced herself to smile. "I hope they all have a wonderful time. And I do understand. Really."

But after they had all gone—Ed left, too, of course, to take Martha home—the smile faded and she stood perfectly still in the middle of the hall for a long time.

Kit called, the minute Joe left her at her own house.

"What do you think?" she asked. "Did she get the idea?"

"Oh, yes—she got it all right," Dodo agreed dully.

"What's the matter? Are you feeling sorry for her? I thought we agreed it was all for the best."

"Sure. We did. Good night, now, Kit." Dodo hung up slowly.

And then the phone rang again, and it was Peg. "I guess Martha knows what a gang really is by now," she said.

"Yes. I guess so. I'm beginning to get the idea myself."

"What do you mean?"

"It's—I'll tell you tomorrow. Only, Peg—when Hank asks you, say yes."

And then she hung up again, and there was Ed, opening the front door and marching toward her menacingly.

"Listen, you," he began, "I've always thought you weren't too bad—for a sister, anyway—but after tonight I . . . Why, Martha has more manners in her little finger than you'll ever have."

"I know, Ed," Dodo said. "I just didn't . . ."

"If you're going to say you just didn't know her—well, you could have *tried* to—instead of . . ."

"I know, Ed," she repeated. He was beginning to look at her oddly, the anger draining out of him at her strange quietness. "But *she* knows *me*, so . . ." She started for the stairs, but halfway up she turned. "Incidentally, it's not good manners to kick a person when she's down. And besides, a girl can change, can't she?" she demanded fiercely.

She could feel Ed's puzzled gaze on her back as she marched up the rest of the stairs. He probably thought she was out of her mind. But it was true. A girl *could* change. Couldn't she? Anyway, she could certainly try.

# When War Came

ANN CHIDESTER

# When War Came

Last summer was before the war, and I was sixteen. All my life had been good—sleep at night and enough time in the day to think and help my folks, and the summers were the best part of living, sun all day and cool winds at night and a boy named Peter Blake visiting at the resort where my aunt lived. He had two years at college and light-blond hair the color of waves when they break, silver and lovely to see, taking the breath away.

My father owns a chain of four hamburger joints—two drive-ins in the city, one on the outskirts, and a fine red-white-and-blue-striped awning affair on the beach. In the summer it is a good business, and in the winter it is only fair as we operate just the two in the city, but there is always enough. My father is a square, handsome man, and his voice comes from his toes. Lots of people have told him he could get into the movies with that funny, deep voice. My mother is a silent woman, not with the silence that is golden but with that peculiar, wise silence that breaks itself only when the time is ripe. All that my mother has ever said has been necessary, true, wise, and without anger or malice. I suppose she could be a very fashionable person, but she does not take the time for it, as she works at the cash register in the main drive-in. She looks very neat and efficient in her striped wash dresses, and my father loves her very much, and I am their only child so it is natural that they would try to make my world very safe, wide, and beautiful for me. It is not just their technique in raising their daughter; it is the way they have and how they believe.

Last summer when I was sixteen, I went to my aunt's place at a summer resort on the coast. It is what I do for almost two months every summer. We had our usual parties and the same crowd, and Peter was nice to me for the first time. I mean, amazed in that utterly simple, male way at finding someone who is wearing lipstick as it should be worn and a new hairdo and nail polish—all these things that come on you during a year when you are changing from adolescent obnoxiousness to being very posh. We drank Cokes and went fishing and listened to news flashes. The only time I remember talking about war was when Peter and I walked past the wharves to the cove to swim. We carried our shoes knotted together by the laces and slung over our shoulders, and the sand was hard-beaten and cool on our feet. We found the separate caves and got into our suits and swam for a while, and afterward we lay on the sand and talked about things.

"Your old man was in the last war, wasn't he?" Peter asked me.

"I guess so."

"You mean you don't know?"

"He never talks about it, but I guess he was."

"I wonder what it was like."

I said, "I wasn't born yet. I wouldn't remember anything about it."

He said, "Neither was I."

I remember that then a plane came over the jutting headlands of rock. We hadn't heard it coming because the surf was beating hard against the rocks north of the cove. The plane was beautiful, plowing up the air, but Peter thought it seemed ominous as it flashed in the sun—like a knife, steel and sharp and terrible.

"This war will be in the air," he said, squinting and watching the plane.

"What war?"

"The war that's going on now—the one we'll be in pretty soon."

"If you're so smart, who'll we be fighting?" I asked him.

"Germany or Japan—almost anyone."

And going home he said, "You know, your mother's a wise woman. She'd know."

"She'd know what?" Although I knew about my mother's wisdom, I did not see what war had to do with it.

"Something—about wars and why men go to them."

"My mother's never been to a war," I said. "How'd she know anything about it?"

"She'd know."

I did not think about war the rest of the summer when I was sixteen.

When I came back and started school again, we heard a lot about war, but it didn't mean much to us. Peter came up from his college some weekends when he could and sometimes he called me up and took me to a movie. One Sunday in December we went to see Claudette Colbert, and when we stopped in at the uptown drive-in, my mother was there and she looked very tired, as if she had been crying. She was filling mustard pots, and my father was behind the grill screen talking with Tony, the boy who fries the burgers. I could hear their voices but not what they said.

"Did you two have fun?" my mother asked.

"Sure," we said and we told her how we had spent the day getting pictures for Peter's album and then going to see Claudette Colbert and eating peanuts in the show. We told her about the dame with the goofy hat who sat in front of us, and she laughed. She likes to hear all those things.

And afterward she said, "We're at war with Japan." It was not a statement. My mother does not go in for things like that. There is always something beyond the words. It was as if this put an end to all fears because there was nothing else to believe in. My mother likes the idea of all men being brothers and no one killing, but when she gets mad, Pops says, she gets mad enough to kill. But she has to be mad for a good reason. When she told us this about Japan, she looked very tired, too tired to be mad, even.

"Well," Peter said suddenly. "I'll be shoving off. I want to check in at the dorm early."

"Come back soon, Peter," my mother said, and they looked at each other and I felt left out, for there is this secret look that comes between people who know they are of the same mind. I had no mind about war. I had never known a war, and when people recalled those fantastic tales of the children of Belgium with their hands chopped off and their bleeding stumps, and how people hated the Germans and spat and called them Huns—well, those things didn't mean much. It sounded like a lot of hooey, and all the people I knew thought it was, too, and they would need more than all that to fight another war. My folks are mild-mannered, wise, secure in their own world, and they are the kind who have to have a reason before they will go into a war.

My father came from behind the screen.

"Hello, baby," he said to me.

"There is a war, Pops," I said.

"Oh, sure, sure," he said slowly, looking at my mother. "But they'll never lick us. We've got something to fight for."

My mother said nothing but kept on filling the mustard pots and wiping them off and putting them on the counter and the little round red tables.

"I'll do that, Mums," I said.

"No," she said. "You'd better go home and do your homework."

"All right," I said, and I walked two blocks down the street to where we lived. I do not know how I felt. It was not a logical feeling, only a restlessness like when you want something and can't have it. I kept thinking about my folks and what my mother would say about the Japanese and this war when she finally broke loose and said something.

At school they were excited, and the boys in the senior class wanted to go right away. One boy named Johnnie Harburg made a speech in assembly. He was the one who always wore bright socks and flashy red suspenders. He was supposed to be a good debater so everyone listened to him. He said it didn't matter how young we were, we could all do something to win the war and he thought we should collect old junk and things. He would put up a bulletin in the main hall so we would know what to collect. Naida Winters, who wears thick lipstick, said she would collect anything in uniform. Some of the kids laughed. Most of us didn't. I think we were all the same —puzzled.

How do you go about a war when you've never seen one except in the movies? I thought war came gradually, not one night when you didn't have it and then the next night when you did. The way the boys talked, you would think it was just learning to fly a plane and wearing two-toned uniforms that cost a lot. They all wanted to go places like Randolph Field and Kelly Field and San Diego. They would do a job of it, they would, and everyone thought how nice they would look in uniform.

After all the speakers on the program had got off their

spiels, Mr. Osberg, the principal, told us this was a serious business but we were a smart nation and could invent and fight and work hard for things we loved. Then we stood up and sang "The Star-Spangled Banner," and most of us knew the words, too. We felt very excited. Going out, Margie Davis asked me to go downtown with her after fifth period as she wanted to get a new pair of saddle shoes. We did not think about the war then.

All through the winter I waited for my mother to say something, but she just looked neater and minded her own business and listened to the radio at night. Usually she listened to music, but after I went to bed I could hear that rat-a-tat-tat that means a wireless and a news flash. I asked Pops if he had been in the last war, and he said yes, he'd been at Château-Thierry and Belleau Wood, but he would not tell me about war.

By spring we were in a nice patriotic fervor at school and saved our allowances for Defense Stamps. Margie Davis' father gave her a War Bond, but mine told me I should do what I could from my allowance and he would do the same from his income. We did not use our car much because of the gasoline rationing, and my father kept the tires wrapped in burlap. At school, they showed us how to put out a magnesium fire-bomb, and the man who did it in the movies was very good and stopped the fire from spreading. It did not seem very exciting to us, only a job to be done. No one was frightened, even in the blackouts we had. If they bombed our city, we knew we could fight them. We loved our city, my father told me, and we would keep it safe.

It was not long before we had got used to being at war. Sometimes we would see lots of soldiers on the streets and we would try to figure out if they were first or second lieutenants. We liked the way they walked and none of them looked frightened, only happy and well-fed and a little lost with nothing to do when they had leaves or furloughs. Maybe their shoes hurt them a little but that was all and, as Margie said, as soon as they got used to marching, their shoes would fit like gloves. This war was not very exciting and we began to think less and less about it.

We thought Colin Kelly was handsome, and his death seemed a glorious thing and not part of the routine of war. Peter dropped in at one of the drive-ins and he was wearing a uniform. He was taking a course called cryptography, which means he would decipher codes. He looked very serious and talked mostly with my mother. But he played the juke box twice and danced with me.

"What were you and Peter talking about, Mums?" I asked.

"Oh—just everything."

"Now, Mums," I said, "I would like to know."

"The spirit of this war. Men must be killed, and you know Peter hates to kill."

"He hates to shoot a duck," I said.

"Yes. So he has to find a reason for killing."

"Did he find it?"

"I think so," she said, but I could tell from her eyes that she was not sure.

"What is a reason?"

She looked at me strangely, as if she would rather not tell me.

She said, "Some people say to stamp out an evil force. Some people say to establish just trade relations. Others say to preserve our way of life and thought. I'm not sure what the reason is." That was all she said.

When summer came again, I did not go to the cottage with my aunt except for a weekend. There was lots of business, and most of the crowd at the resort had changed. Carlie Miller was being married to Ted; and Pops said, since she was just my age, she seemed awfully young to be married. War pushed people into it, and then afterward they were sorry. Young kids got a sort of marrying fever. My mother just looked at him, and finally she said, "War makes children cease to be children any longer."

Peter could not come to the weekend party, and I was just as glad. It was different. We were different. Hank Darrow, who has always been one of the most truly sophisticated boys I've ever known, was going to be a flyer. He did not talk about it much, but he acted funny. Margie said it was as if we didn't have any tomorrow and wanted to cram everything into that one weekend. Some of the fellows wanted to go to the Beach Tavern which is a horrible place and forbidden to most of us, but we took the dare and went. Fatso Brown got very drunk and cried and said he had to diet to get into a uniform. Usually, Fatso is fun and tells funny stories and does the Mischa Auer act, leaping on furniture and pretending to be an ape. Poor Fatso. He sort of made me sick. And then Hank drank too much. When I was sixteen, the summer before, they drank only Cokes.

When Hank and I danced, I closed my eyes and he turned around and around and then we went out on the beach to look at the moon. Hank is usually very proper, but he was not this time. He wasn't Hank Darrow any more, just a fellow who drank too much and wanted to get fresh.

There were other things, too, that weekend, that didn't happen the summer before. And the way some of the boys took to their uniforms, some of them quiet and rugged and some of them as if it were just a lot of fun. Well, you didn't know. The war didn't mean much even then.

But I was glad to be back in town, and then Mums asked me if I didn't want to take a cash register at the Number Two drive-in because on Saturday nights the soldiers were as thick as bees in there.

"Oh," I said. "Mums, you're a peach. I would love to do that."

Number Two is in the very center of town and, if I do say so myself, it is the neatest drive-in in this whole city. My father designed it, and it is circular, made of white stucco trimmed in blue, and there is a swell place to dance and all the girls have blue-and-white uniforms. We sell more burgers there than in any of the other three shops.

The soldiers started coming in about seven-thirty. They were very neat and they did not know what to do with themselves. They were tanned and hard, and they could eat more burgers than a ditch-digger on a twenty-hour shift. The juke box was playing all the time. A few of them had girls, but most of them wrote post cards or played cards and shot dice or matched pennies.

One lieutenant named Red liked to tell bright stories the way Bob Burns does—slow drawl and dopey things about his people from Michigan. Everyone laughed at him. The rest of them liked him and bought him burgers and even double flips, which are the most expensive ice-cream affairs we have, very rich and gooey but nice to eat if you are hungry. This Red was hungry all the time.

Pops would drop in on his rounds and take over the cash register for me so I could dance with Red. He had very nice manners and said he would look up Peter if he had a chance.

I went to the Number Two regularly on Saturday night, and during the week I worked at the beach. The same soldiers came to the Number Two and played the juke box. It was fun for me, too, as we could wisecrack over the counter or act plain silly. Then they began to change; new ones came, and the old ones were gone. Gone to Hawaii, Australia, the New Hebrides—these names were like the ones Pops told me, lovely, strange, and they made me think of Shalimar, Kashmir, sandalwood, Java.

"Where is Red?" I asked when he had not come for several Saturday nights. I asked the one named Pud.

He shrugged. "Who knows?"

"You mean you don't know where he is?"

He grinned and looked at me with old eyes and said slowly, "Look, Joan, this is war, honey."

A few weeks later I was sitting in the beach drive-in during the slump hour reading a magazine. I turned the page, and there was Red looking at me with his hair all sort of blowy in the wind and the same funny expression on his face as if he were asking for the -teenth hamburger. The magazine said he was dead—his plane had been downed by the enemy, and his family lived in Iron Mountain, Michigan, where his father was a carpenter. He was twenty-two.

It was like Colin Kelly but different. It was real, for I knew Red as I knew Peter Blake and Hank Darrow and Fatso Brown. War, then, was when people you knew were killed.

"What—what about Peter and all those other fellows?" I asked my mother.

She smiled and I could see her face in the mirror as she combed her hair. "We don't know. We can't understand beyond a certain point, for we are not a war-minded people. But we do know we like our way of life."

"Will it ever be as it was—I mean the way it used to be up at the cottage and all of us dancing and drinking Cokes? The way it was before?" I felt like crying, but that seemed silly.

"Do you think it will be the same?" she asked.

I shook my head. But I was not afraid—only amazed. Red must have believed he was right to do what he did—and Peter—and all the rest of them, and Pops, too, when he did it. It will not be the same—I know. Better, though, I think.

And this fall I am older—much older—and already almost everything looks different.

# Web of Dreams

MARY BRINKER POST

# Web of Dreams

Lorna's desk was the last one in the row next to the windows. Her French book was open before her, but as soon as Angelo Rizzonelli got up to translate the first paragraph, Lorna's gaze wandered to the window. She could see a square of bright blue sky, a white cloud like a puff of smoke, and the heavy, leafy boughs of the elm that grew beside the school. But that was not what she really saw.

She saw a tall, slim girl walking gracefully over a broad, green lawn. This girl looked very much like Lorna except that she wasn't dressed in a plain sweater and skirt but in an exotic silk-jersey sun suit, and she had longer lashes, more curves, and a proud, free carriage instead of the way Lorna usually walked. She was laughing over her bare, tanned shoulder at the handsome young man in bathing trunks who followed her. Two other men stood watching, and one of them said to the other, "That's Lorna Bixby. She's the most popular deb of the season. She's had dozens of proposals, and she's going to marry the star halfback on the Yale football team. They're going to Bermuda on their honeymoon."

Lorna smiled faintly and cupped her chin in her hand.

Angelo Rizzonelli sat down, and the teacher called on Sarah Weinstein to continue the translation. Lorna was dimly aware of this, but she didn't glance at her French book. Another scene flashed before her bemused gaze. The same girl was sitting at a soda fountain, daintily sipping a Coke. She was wearing a beautifully tailored tweed suit and a string of real pearls. A man dashed up to her and said, "Pardon me, Miss Bixby, but I'm a talent scout for MGM. The minute I saw you, I knew you were just the type I've been looking for to star opposite Guy Madison in his latest picture. Will you come to Hollywood for a screen test?"

"Lorna Bixby, if you can stop looking out the window for a few minutes, I'd like you to translate the next paragraph."

"Lorna!" whispered the girl in the opposite seat. "She means you. Come out of your trance, dopey."

Lorna came to with a start, fumbled with her book, got to her feet, dropped her pencil, retrieved it, and started to translate the wrong paragraph.

"Sarah just translated that, Lorna," said Miss Hodges impatiently, with a cold, frowning stare. "You'd better stay after school this afternoon and write out the whole page. Perhaps that will teach you to pay attention in class."

A titter rippled over the class and Lorna sat down, her cheeks burning. After the last period she came back to the French room and got out *Sans Famille* to write out the page. Miss Hodges came in while she was working on it and stood beside her, a puzzled expression on her face.

"I don't understand it, Lorna," she said, not unkindly. "You used to be one of my best students. But all this semester you've been so different. You never seem to be paying attention."

"I'm sorry, Miss Hodges," murmured Lorna, feeling ashamed and sort of futile.

"What's the matter, my dear? Don't you feel well, or is there something troubling you?" Miss Hodges leaned on Lorna's desk and gazed earnestly into her face. Lorna blushed and shook her head, smiling in embarrassment.

"Oh, I'm OK. I'll try to do better," was all she said.

How could she tell her teacher that everything was different now, since Dad and Mother were divorced? How could she explain the way she felt—as if the bottom had dropped out of the world and she didn't know where she belonged, no longer safe or sure of anything? You couldn't tell that to anyone, not even Dad or Mother. You just kept it inside and tried to forget it, pretended you were a different person or something—anything to make you feel sure of yourself again. In your dreams you weren't scared or lonely or shy or awkward; you were beautiful, popular, successful. In your dreams everything worked out perfectly.

She walked home alone. School would be out in another two weeks and the long summer stretched before her. Other years she'd looked forward to vacation eagerly. She and Dad and Mother used to have such fun in the summer, going on picnics, spending a month at the beach cottage, taking drives to the mountains. Once they drove clear out to Yellowstone Park. But this summer—Mother had a job now and she hadn't been at the store long enough to get a vacation. They no longer lived in the pleasant roomy house on the Drive. That was sold, and she and her mother had a tiny three-room apartment.

Oh, why did everything have to change? thought Lorna desperately. Why couldn't we have gone on just as we used to? What happened and why? She guessed she'd never know the answers. There never were any fights or scenes between her parents. On the surface, and as far as she could tell, everything had been all right. And then one day her mother had told her that she was leaving her father.

"We feel it's the only thing to do, Lorna," was all her mother had said. "It's not anything you could understand. But we can't go on living together."

So they were divorced, and now Lorna hadn't seen her father for six months.

Taking the short cut through the park, Lorna nearly bumped into a tall, blond boy who was carrying two tennis rackets. She'd been so lost in her thoughts she hadn't seen him coming.

"Oh, I'm sorry," she said, blushing in confusion.

"It's OK. My fault, anyhow," he said, laughing. "Hey, aren't you Lorna Bixby?"

She met his bright, blue eyes shyly. "Yes."

He grinned at her. "Well, I'll be seeing you," and he swung over to the tennis courts.

Still blushing with embarrassment, she hurried toward home. So he knew her name! She didn't suppose he'd ever noticed her. She knew all about him. He was Jerry Mann, captain of the basketball team, president of the Student Council. He had the lead in the senior play, too. Her eyes grew dreamy, and she began to smile. She saw a crowded dance floor, heard sweet, slow music, saw herself in a white net dress, a flower in her hair. She was dancing with the tall, blond boy with the bright, blue eyes. Someone said as they swept by, "There's Lorna Bixby with Jerry Mann. They're going steady now, did you know?"

When she ran up the three flights of stairs to the apartment, her eyes were still shining with her dream. There were several letters in the mailbox, most of them for her mother and one letter for her. It was from her father's office in Chicago. She opened it quickly and read the short, typewritten note from her father.

Dear Lorna,

I had been looking forward to having you spend the summer with me. As I believe you know, the court allows me to have you part of the year; and since I didn't wish to take you out of school, I arranged with your mother to have you for the summer months. Unfortunately, my dear, I have to go on an extended sales survey and it will be impossible to take you with me. So I have arranged for you to spend July and August at a very fine girls' camp in the Adirondacks. I hope this will be satisfactory with both you and your mother.

Affectionately,
Dad

When her mother came home that night, Lorna showed her the letter. "Why, I think that will be lovely, dear," Mrs. Bixby said with a tired smile. "There's nothing very exciting for you to do here all summer. And I can't get away for even a few days' vacation."

"But, Mother, I don't think I should leave you. I ought to get a job, too, and help out," cried Lorna. It terrified her to think of going to a camp with a lot of strange girls, trying to make friends, trying to fit in.

"I wouldn't think of letting you, dear. We don't need the money that badly. And it's not been very pleasant for you since—since the divorce. You'll have a wonderful time. Really, you will."

Her father met her in Chicago and they had one whole day together. He tried very hard to give her a fine time, took her to the best restaurants for lunch and dinner, drove her along Michigan Boulevard, showed her the sights, bought her a huge box of candy, a new bathing suit, an armful of magazines. But it was such a strange feeling, being there with him without Mother, being careful not to mention her too much or to bring up things they used to do, which made a queer, strained look come over his face. Lorna was really glad when he put her on the train, kissed her good-by, squeezed her shoulder, and said, "Have a fine time and write and tell me all about it, honey." She thought he looked relieved, too, as he hurried down the train aisle.

Camp Adventure was a splendid, well-equipped place set on the edge of a blue lake, ringed about by green, wooded hills. The tents were roomy, clean, and comfortable. The food was excellent, and there was plenty of it. The counselors were brisk and pleasant. But it was just as Lorna feared. She didn't fit in; she couldn't seem to make friends.

Most of the girls had been there before, and they hailed each other with cries of glee. Lorna's three tentmates had known each other in school. They chattered endlessly about the fun they'd had together, scrapes they'd got into. Lorna sat on her bed and read the magazines her father had bought her. As she listened to their happy voices she wished she were home in the hot little apartment.

During the day it wasn't so bad. They went on hikes and canoe trips. They swam. Lorna was a good swimmer. It was about the only thing she could do very well, and she liked to swim away from the others, to practice new strokes, or just to float on her back, lapped by the cool water, as she stared up at the clear blue sky.

But in the afternoon rest periods and in the evenings before taps, the loneliness, the sense of being shut out and insecure closed in on her again until her heart seemed ready to burst. One afternoon when she came in from a hike and threw herself on her bed, the other girls, Anne, Betsy, and Joan, were reading letters.

"Listen to what Bill says," cried Joan, giggling.

"Who's Bill?" demanded Anne.

"Oh, didn't I tell you? He's my latest flame. Oh, he's darling. Dark hair and wonderful brown eyes. He's going away to school in the fall and he's already asked me up for the Thanksgiving dance."

That started them off. They all began to talk about their boy friends, and they listened eagerly while Joan read Bill's letter. Lorna was watching them when Anne looked up and met her gaze.

"Hey, Lorna," she said in a teasing tone, "why so silent? Aren't you going to tell us about your boy friend?"

It was on the tip of Lorna's tongue to say, "I haven't one," when Betsy laughed and murmured, "Maybe she hasn't a boy friend."

Lorna's face grew hot and she looked away. For a moment there was silence in the room, and then she heard herself say in a dreamy voice, "Yes, I have a boy friend. He's tall and blond and he has the nicest blue eyes. He's captain of the basketball team and president of the Student Council at high school. Oh, and he had the lead in the senior play."

All the girls were looking at her curiously. It was as if they'd never seen her before. "Well," said Joan breathlessly, "he does sound solid. What's his name?"

"His name is Jerry Mann," said Lorna in a clear, confident voice.

That night there was a masquerade party in the assembly hall. Lorna hadn't brought a costume, so she'd decided not to go. But Joan dug a Spanish shawl out of her trunk and Anne offered her black peasant dirndl. Betsy lent her gypsy earrings and helped Lorna make up. As they started off for the hall in the dark, Joan linked arms with Lorna and began to sing one of the camp songs.

It was very curious, but from then on, Lorna belonged. All because of a lie. Only, somehow, she never thought of it as that. It was as if she had merely put her dreams into words; and since her dreams had become more real to her than everyday life, it didn't seem wrong.

She told the girls about going to the Senior Ball with Jerry, about dancing with him, about the white net dress, about his gardenias in her hair. It was easy to talk to them now, because she was no longer shy, awkward Lorna Bixby, but the other Lorna, the one for whom everything turned out perfectly.

Now she didn't go off by herself to swim, but swam with the others and won their admiration and respect for her strong, swift stroke, her clean, poised diving.

"We're going to have a swimming meet in two weeks with guests and relatives invited, Lorna," said the swimming counselor. "You ought to turn out for it. Your only real competitor is Helen Swanson."

"Lorna can beat Helen any old day," cried Joan loyally, and Lorna felt warm and proud of Joan's friendship, her faith in her.

One afternoon not long before the meet, as Lorna and her tentmates lay on the beach after swimming, Helen came over and sat down with them. As usual, the talk had swung around to boys.

"Bill's coming up for the swimming meet," announced Joan proudly.

"Oh, good!" Betsy laughed. "Now we'll find out if he's as wonderful as you say he is."

"Why don't you ask Jerry up?" Joan turned to Lorna.

"Jerry who?" asked Helen.

"Oh, Lorna's super boy friend from Springfield. What's his last name, Lorna?"

"Mann," said Lorna.

"Jerry Mann? And he lives in Springfield?" Helen looked suddenly interested. Lorna nodded, and Joan said eagerly, "Do you know him, Helen?"

Helen laughed. "I'll say I do. He's my cousin."

"Well, it's a small world!" cried Betsy. "Tell us about him. Give us an unprejudiced version. Is he tall and blond and handsome? Star athlete, big man about school, and all that? Lorna's been raving about him for weeks."

"He's pretty smooth. All the girls are crazy about him." Helen looked at Lorna curiously. "But I didn't know he went with you, Lorna. I thought he was Doris Lane's steady."

Hot color washed up over Lorna's face, and her stomach felt queer and empty. All at once she was back in her old world, insecure and frightened. She looked at the interested faces of her friends who were waiting for her to speak. They liked her, they admired and believed in her. But it was all false.

She swallowed hard, stammered, "Oh, he went with her last year, I guess," and then she got up and put on her bathing cap again. "I'm too hot. Let's go for a dip."

They all followed her into the water and the moment passed. But as they went up to dress, Helen gave her a thoughtful look, and Lorna couldn't meet her eyes.

The morning of the swimming meet the girls came away from breakfast talking excitedly about the day that was before them.

"Oh, Lorna," called Helen, as they passed her tent. She ran down the path, waving a letter. "Guess who's coming today?" Lorna stared at her, uncomfortable under her direct gaze. "Jerry. Jerry Mann. I invited him as a surprise for you." Her tentmates crowded around her eagerly, but Lorna stood as if turned to stone.

"Now you've *got* to win the meet!" cried Joan.

Lorna couldn't say a word. Suddenly she felt trapped. She turned and ran down the path to her tent. All she wanted to do was run and hide. How could she face her friends and *Jerry?* She gasped at the thought of being confronted with him, of Helen's mocking smile, her friends' disgust when they found out what she'd done. She couldn't swim in the meet. She'd simply go for a walk in the woods and stay there until it was all over and the visitors had gone. Then she'd pack her things, pretend she was ill, and go home.

Before the girls reached the tent, Lorna was gone. She took the path that led deep into the woods. She climbed until she was hot and tired, and then she lay down on the pine-strewn earth and tried to shut out the painful reality of her thoughts. She closed her eyes, waiting for the dream to come and take away her shame and humiliation.

But nothing happened. All she could see was Helen's accusing gaze as she came toward her with the letter, and the look that would be on Anne's and Joan's and Betsy's faces when Jerry told them the truth. Then she knew that this time she couldn't hide in her dream world and she couldn't hide up here on the hill.

There was only one thing for her to do. She must go down to camp, tell the girls that she was a liar and a fraud. She'd go home then, because they wouldn't want her at camp. She'd go home and face the real facts of her life and try to be brave and honest, and maybe someday things would work out better for her. Not the way they did in her dreams, because now she saw that they never would. She wasn't ever going to be a movie star, or a glamorous deb. She wasn't even going to dance with a boy like Jerry Mann.

She was just a nice, not bad-looking girl, rather shy and awkward, but there were things about her people liked when they got to know her. There were even things she did better than others—such as swimming. She'd have to be content with what she was and with what she had.

But when she reached the tent the girls didn't give her a chance to tell them.

"Holy mackerel!" cried Joan, grabbing her and thrusting a bathing suit in her hands. "Where have you been? We've looked all over for you. You've got to get down to the float. Miss Peterson wants everybody there by a quarter to two."

"And it's one-thirty now!" shrieked Betsy, dancing around her. "If you aren't at the float on time, you'll be disqualified and can't compete and I've already bet three people my charm bracelet that you'll win."

In a daze, Lorna undressed and put on her bathing suit. She'd had no idea that she'd been gone so long. Her hands shook as she fastened her halter, and she thought, I ought to drop out of the meet. I'll never be able to swim, feeling like this. But she'd already done enough to her friends. She couldn't let them down on this. She'd just have to do the best she could.

Helen and the others who were competing were already on the float when Lorna got there. "Gosh," cried Helen, "we thought you were lost or something! Gee, I'm glad you're all right." She put out her hand. "Good luck, Lorna, and may the best girl win."

As Lorna shook hands, she realized that Helen was really glad to see her, that she'd been worried about her.

She knows the truth, thought Lorna, but she's sorry she called my bluff.

Suddenly Lorna smiled, just before Miss Peterson blew the warning whistle. Don't worry, Helen, she wanted to say, *I'm all right*. I've been walking around in a dream for a long time, but I'm wide awake now. It's not going to be easy to tell the girls the truth, but I can do it. If I've lost their friendship, then I'll have to win it back. And I can do that, too, because I think they like me now for myself, not for anything I made up.

Helen was beside her, poised as she was for the take-off, and she said in a low voice that no one but Lorna could hear, "I didn't tell Jerry what you said about going with him, Lorna. But I did tell him I'd made a new friend up here who was pretty special and that I'd get him a date with her for the dance tonight."

Lorna glanced at her swiftly. "You mean *me*, Helen?"

"Sure," said Helen, with a warm smile. "Who else?"

"Then you knew all along that I'd made it up about Jerry and me?" gasped Lorna.

Helen nodded.

"And you don't hate me for it?"

"Gosh, no. Jerry's such a swell cousin, I wouldn't blame anyone for dreaming about him."

Lorna's heart leaped, and suddenly she felt strong and free. If Helen didn't hate her for letting her dreams get out of hand, maybe the other girls wouldn't, either!

The starting whistle blew a shrill blast. The crowd of spectators cheered. And as Lorna hit the water in a clean, shallow, racing dive she knew she was going to swim as she never had before, and she knew, too, that she was going to win.

# The Dress

GERTRUDE CRAMPTON

# The Dress

It was still there, now in the corner window of Campbell's Dress Shop and cunningly set off by navy blue to make it bloom all the more. Liz Young sighed with relief and hurried on to cash her pay check. It was still there, the date dress of all date dresses. It was a perfect color—yellow. Just the yellow that a mother or an aunt would admire, saying, "It will do things for you, dear."

But whoever had designed the dress hadn't had mothers and aunts in mind. She'd had Liz Young in mind, and Robin Perry. She'd thought of Liz's lithe slimness when she had artfully shirred the side seams of the snug top. She'd known of Robin's love of dancing, and had gored a skirt for twirling. She'd known they often sang snatches of chorus as they danced effortlessly, and she'd sprinkled black grace notes in a melodic sweep. Oh, it was the dress for Liz Young, and as soon as she cashed her check she was going to own that wicked little buttercup of a dress.

Mother had been opposed to Liz's working after school.

"If you'd wait until summer," she'd said, "I'd have nothing to say against it."

The dress would be gone long before summer. It would be gone in less than a month, for wasn't the greatest of all the name bands coming to Lambertville just three weeks from Saturday for a one-night stand?

The neatly printed card under the dress notified the passing parade that it was available for $19.95. Nineteen-ninety-five was a lot to pay for such a butterfly dress, but somebody in the high school crowd could surely persuade a grumbling father that she just *had* to have the dress for the dance at the Westmoreland Hotel. Just had to, if she was to do justice to Kenny Maitland's music; just had to, if she wanted to make a splash; just had to, if she was to be happy. Liz knew all about fathers and she'd have got the $19.95 from her own mock-grumbling dad if it hadn't been for the war. The war had changed Daddy from an easy-going, adoring grumbler to a hard-eyed, we'll-have-no-nonsense father. At least, he was a we'll-have-no-nonsense father about money. Robin said his dad was that way, too, nowadays.

"It's because they were in the last war," Robin explained. "They can't fight in this one, but they're awfully stubborn about home-front stuff. You know, War Bonds, wear it out, make it do."

"And don't have any fun," Liz finished.

It hadn't been too bad, until suddenly there was the dress. And Liz knew that Daddy would never give her the money—not for Kenny Maitland's band, not for her first hotel dance, not for Robin Perry, who'd be going away one of these days to learn to be a navigator.

"Not for the whole United States Army Air Force," Liz could almost hear Daddy say.

It was on a Thursday afternoon that Liz had seen the dress in the teen department, known Daddy wouldn't give her the money, mourned hopelessly, and had her great idea all in the space of five minutes. More purposeful than any businessman in Lambertville, she strode to the nearest newsstand for a Coke and a fast glance at the want ads. Like an answer to a prayer, there it was, the next to the last ad. "Wanted: High school boy or girl to work afternoons and Saturdays. Franklin Printing & Engraving Co."

Franklin Printing & Engraving was just around the corner, and Liz was there as fast as her shoes would move.

"I came about the job," she said hesitantly to the old man who shuffled up to her. He looked *ninety!*

"Oh, the job," he mumbled. "You'll need to see Mr. Fred." And he led her into a cubbyhole office cluttered with cuts and proofs and papers. "I'll get him."

Mr. Fred was ancient, too, and pleasant but firm. The job began just as soon as she could get downtown from school, and no fiddle-faddle on the way. Saturdays she must be there promptly at nine. Liz thought fleetingly of luxurious bed-lolling on Saturday mornings. She would be paid $10.00 a week.

Oh, golly! thought Liz. Ten dollars for all that work! Bus fare to come out of it, and Saturday lunch. It takes a lot of doing to get $20.00 for a dress.

Aloud she said, "That isn't very much money."

Mr. Fred looked at her strangely for a moment, and Liz thought he was going to yell. But all he said was, "That's more than forty cents an hour. We think it quite generous pay for inexperienced help."

Forty cents an hour did seem fair pay for an inexperienced girl, even though it took such a lot of hours to come out to $20.00.

"I'll take the job," Liz decided briskly. "That is, if you want to hire me."

Mr. Fred said he'd hire her, but he looked as though he

didn't expect much. In fact, he was pretty gloomy about everything and muttered about all the help problem in general.

"See you Monday afternoon," Liz assured him blithely as she left. And she could have sworn he said, "Oh yeah!" but that, of course, was just imagination. Well, she'd be there only three weeks, till she earned enough for the dress.

Liz took up the subject of jobs in general and hers in particular at supper that night.

"I won't have it," Mother protested. "I just won't have it, Elizabeth."

And while Liz thought despairingly of the dress, who should come galloping to her aid but unpredictable Daddy.

"Don't be too hasty, Jan," he said. "This is not a bad idea Elizabeth has. She's doing good work at school, and a part-time job shouldn't affect her grades. It isn't as though she'd have to work nights, and I know the people at Franklin Printing very well. Fine, well-established, old, conservative firm."

And that's no stuff, added Liz mentally.

"The thing is," Daddy went on, "lots of these small firms are going to be pushed out of business unless the youngsters help. The young men are gone, and the defense factories have grabbed off most of the rest. Not that I blame the big war plants or the people who work in them, but little businesses can't afford to match defense pay. Yet if they don't get help some place, they'll go to the wall. I'm all for Liz's job, and I think she's a mighty patriotic girl."

A ray of hope for the dress shot through Liz's mind.

"Well," Mother gave in, "I hadn't thought of it in quite that way. If your teachers agree, Elizabeth, and if you keep your schoolwork up, I guess it would be a patriotic thing to do."

Before the bell rang the next morning, Liz had the permission of every one of her teachers—not only permission but an enthusiastic blessing. During her first study hour she went to the principal's office. Mr. Bell looked at her almost respectfully as she stated her errand.

"Elizabeth," he said at last, "I guess I owe you an apology. I had you ticketed as a nice young girl, but rather . . ."

"Featherbrained," offered Liz helpfully.

Mr. Bell smiled. "Ah, that is not, perhaps, just the adjective I would have selected, but it is extremely descriptive. Yes, ah, featherbrained.

"Now I find you to be fully aware of one of the grave problems facing all communities. Not only aware of it, but ready to take decisive action. Well, go to it, Elizabeth." Mr. Bell nodded dismissal. "Not many girls would take a routine job just to keep the wheels of Lambertville turning."

Liz hurried down the hall. The wheels of Lambertville indeed. The only thing she wanted to keep turning was the dress, and she'd swirl that at a dizzy pace when Kenny Maitland sounded off with his mighty licorice stick.

The grapevine at school was a powerful thing. Better than radar, Robin contended. The crowd knew almost as much about Liz's job as Liz herself did when they met at lunch.

"Who'd have thought our Liz would be the next patriot?" Dick James greeted her with mock awe.

"Who, indeed!" echoed Sally, and flounced a little. "Especially in a spot where she can't wear a uniform."

Good gosh, she's jealous! Liz thought. Jealous of me and my ten-dollar job. Wait until she sees me in the dress!

"Shove down," whispered Robin. Liz obligingly shoved until she and Robin were separated from the rest of the crowd by a few feet of bench.

"I just wanted to tell you," Robin kept his voice low, "that I think I'll keep on with my paper route. It probably seems sort of kiddish, but I've built that route up since grade school, and it pays off pretty well. Besides, my customers are used to me."

"My goodness, Robin, you don't have to explain to me!"

"Well, I just thought you might be wondering why a big lout like me isn't taking a man-sized job. I was thinking during French that as long as you're tied up anyway now in the afternoons, I could get the papers around and bone up on a little math besides. Maybe get old Bell to help me out with some astronomy." Robin looked at her hopefully.

Why, Robin was discussing things with her! Liz was tongue-tied. She and Robin had played around together practically since they had graduated to rompers, but this was the first time that he had, well, *explained.*

"Sounds like a firm plan," she murmured.

All this respect, all this my-how-Elizabeth-has-grown-up, just because she was going to work at Franklin Printing for a while to get the dress. Of course, to be perfectly honest, Liz admitted to herself, she hadn't told anyone about the dress. The way the crowd acted and the serious way Robin talked, she just couldn't tell.

The job at Franklin Printing & Engraving turned out pretty much as Liz expected it would. She had to do the chasing down to the stock room for a gross of pencils and a ream of this and a ream of that. The only thing that really annoyed her was Mr. Fred. He had grunted when she showed up for work the first day, and he had grunted every afternoon since.

Still, the respectful admiration she got from the crowd and from Mr. Bell sort of made up for the dullness of the job. They all thought it was fine and exciting, and even Daddy seemed to think she must be having a high old time, for he was always asking how his little tycoon was getting along.

Liz was never quite sure whether Mother actually knew

about the dress. Liz had been admiring it one Saturday when who should be reflected in Campbell's glass but Mother.

"Pretty," murmured Mother. "That color would do things for you, Elizabeth."

That was all Mother said, but Mother didn't join in on the family laughter when Daddy talked about his little tycoon. Mother seemed to be waiting, and there was a watchful look in the back of her eyes.

No, she never said anything, not even this morning, when Daddy peeked over the newspaper and said, "This is the big day, isn't it, baby?"

"This is it," Liz agreed.

"What do you say we make it a real party, Jan? I mean, let's take the kids to the Westmoreland for dinner before the dance?"

"In the main dining room, for dinner?" Liz begged. What a stir the dress would make!

"In the main dining room. You've worked hard for three weeks, honey, without a complaint and without missing a day. I think you've earned a treat. How about it, Jan?"

Then, if ever, Liz expected Mother to break the news, to say, "You've got this all wrong. Liz isn't working for Franklin. She's working for a yellow dress in Campbell's window." Instead, Mother had smilingly agreed that dinner at the hotel would be a grand treat. But the watchful look was still in her eyes as Liz kissed her good-by and ran for her bus.

"Well, it's all over now," Liz concluded, as she hurried to the bank with her ten-dollar check. In fifteen minutes the dress would be tucked carefully in tissue. Then she'd tell grunting Mr. Fred to find himself another helper. The watchful look in Mother's eyes would be answered. But golly, who would give up the dress just because of a look in somebody's eyes! It wasn't reasonable.

The teller handed Liz $10.00, and she folded it carefully around the other bills she'd worked so hard to save. This was it! Liz left the bank in great, surging excitement.

The Saturday crowds eddied and drifted past Campbell's and the little island Liz and the dress made as they admired each other in the window. The highly polished glass reflected them, but Liz saw nothing but the dress. Someone bumped her elbow gently and said, "Excuse me," and Liz saw that it was a young man. The apologetic smile of his wife signaled, "Excuse him. He can't see." Uniformed men hurried by. A vague voice remarked, "You got to admit the British women and kids can sure take it." And another replied sharply, "So could our women and kids if they had to." Nothing happened there in front of the dress. Nothing dramatic or sudden or vital. Nothing at all, really. Not even Liz Young knew why she turned on her heel and plodded back to the bank to say sourly, "Oh, give me a War Bond."

There was time enough, and money enough, to get something to brighten up the blue dress she'd have to wear for the thousandth time. Without much enthusiasm, Liz picked up a flowered weskit. She'd bought the bond, but she didn't have to like doing it.

All I need now, she thought as she turned in at Franklin's, is for Mr. Fred to grunt.

Mr. Fred looked at his watch.

"Back from lunch right on time, Elizabeth, I see." Well, so he could speak as well as grunt. "Isn't this the night the great Kenny Maitland plays at the Westmoreland?"

When Liz agreed that he had his dates straight, Mr. Fred bumbled on, "I expect you'd like to get off a little early? You young women seem to need quite some time to get fixed up."

Not me, thought Liz. Won't take me any time at all to crawl into that blue rag.

"I've arranged for you to get off at three-thirty. That ought to give you time enough to get prettied up for your young man. I, ah, I never thought you'd go through with the job. Didn't expect you that first Monday, and when you came, I thought you'd stick it out a week. Then I figured two weeks. Now you've been here three and still going strong." Mr. Fred peered at her over the rims of his glasses. "You are still going strong, aren't you?"

"Yes," replied Liz gently, "I'm still going strong, I guess."

"Fine!" beamed Mr. Fred. "Fine! You're a real help, Liz. Strong young arms and speedy young feet and a gay young laugh. We need you.

"I talk too much. Bad habit. Now, you shoot along at half past three. And have fun, Liz."

Mother came out of the kitchen when Liz opened the front door.

"Mr. Fred, the old duck, let me off early," Liz explained.

"Oh? That was nice." Mother eyed the package.

"Got a weskit to try to help my blue along tonight," Liz said. "Bought a bond today."

Mother said, "That was a fine investment, Elizabeth, dear. A very fine investment."

And Liz knew that was all Mother would ever say.

As the four of them—Mother and Daddy and Liz and Robin—walked down the street to the hotel for dinner, there was no way of dodging Campbell's window, or the dress waiting in lonely grandeur. Liz took the bull by the horns. She couldn't spend the rest of her life carefully not looking in Campbell's.

"That's the dress I almost bought for tonight," she said.

"Oh, that!" Robin looked it over. "Pretty, all right. But

I'm glad you bought the one you've got on. It does something for you, Liz."

"I'm for blue, too," said Daddy.

Liz opened her mouth. Mother reached across that dumb Robin Liz was ready to murder and patted Liz's clenched hands.

"These men!" Mother chuckled. "These men!"

And while Daddy and Robin stood helplessly by and wondered what in the world they'd done now, Mother and Liz dissolved into ridiculous, silly, companionable laughter.

# Sweet Victory

ADELE DE LEEUW

# Sweet Victory

"Coming to the meeting after school, Redhead?" asked Peter, as he joined her on the corner. Sally Mason nodded happily. It was swell to be strolling along the street again with Peter, to have him calling her Redhead, the way he used to. Her hair was brown; it was her temper that had given her the nickname—and lots of other names besides. Redhead was by far the nicest one. It was her temper that had driven Peter away. For a while—a terribly long while, it seemed—she had been afraid that she'd really gone too far, that he wouldn't come back. And she couldn't have borne that.

But here he was. Talking the way he always had, asking questions, looking down at her, from his lean height, with sparkling blue eyes. At first he'd been a little stiff, and so had she. She didn't know how much he remembered of that awful scene. But when he said nothing about it, she knew he didn't want to remember—just as she didn't. It made her hot and cold all over. Maybe, after all, they could get back on the old footing.

"There's a lot to be done," Peter was saying. He took her arm and pulled her back. "Hey, want to walk right through a red light?"

She laughed. "I was thinking."

"Dangerous business. But seriously, you'd better start thinking about that meeting. You know why I called it, don't you?"

"Yes," she said. "Something's *got* to be done. But oh, Peter, I don't see what we can do."

"Don't give up the ship before we get out of the bay," he advised.

"Why, I wasn't!" She turned to face him. "What a silly thing to say!"

"It wathn't ath thilly ath it thounds." He grinned at her. "Everybody . . ."

But the color rode high in her face. She stopped and stamped her foot.

"Don't you dare mock me, Peter Harwood!" she stormed.

His eyes darkened. "Easy, there!"

"I'm sick and tired of your making fun of me!"

"It's a fascinating lisp," he drawled. "It sort of gets me."

She never lisped except when she was angry or excited and he knew it. He *was* making fun of her, teasing her. She hated it!

Something perverse and hurt inside her made her say, "I *don't* lisp . . ." and it came out "lithp." Furiously she threw her books on the ground. "You can just apologize yourself. It's time you grew up."

He let her books lie. "It's time *you* did," he returned. "And the sooner the quicker." She was horrified to see him walking away, and with a determined set to his shoulders. She waited. But he did not turn.

She couldn't believe it. It had happened again. And what was it all about? Oh, darn her old temper, darn it, darn it! It was always getting her into trouble. Everything seemed to be going along all right, then some little thing happened—like this—and she could feel the blood rushing up to her head, and before she knew it, words came tumbling out—and she'd had another quarrel with somebody. Somebody like Peter.

Through a blur of tears she stared down at her books lying on the grass. I won't cry, I won't! she said fiercely to herself. But she knew Peter wouldn't come back this time. It was once too often. She felt as if she had a bag of stones in her chest. I could kick myself, she thought gloomily, picking up the scattered books. But would it do any good?

Probably not. She'd had a quick temper for as long as she could remember. People didn't like it, she knew, but somehow she couldn't stop. She'd tried, oh, she *had* tried! But it came like a flash, always, and often she was surprised at herself. She couldn't know that she had lashed out, hurt somebody's feelings, upset the applecart, until it was all over. And then, of course, what could she do? She wasn't going to go around all the time saying, "I'm sorry." If people couldn't make allowances for her, they'd have to leave her alone.

She walked wearily up the school steps. Lately, though, it seemed as if more and more of the people she really cared about were leaving her alone. Amy had got huffy, and didn't ask her over any more; Catherine went around with her nose in the air; Doris had left her out of the round robin dance; and now Peter . . . She could hardly lift one foot in front of the other. And now Peter! That hurt. Peter counted more than any of the others, more than she'd ever realized.

At first she thought she wouldn't go to the meeting. But everybody would be there; they'd think it queer if she stayed away. And it *was* important. They had a real grievance this time. Peter had called the meeting—Peter was president of the class—to hash things over. They had to find a way out and do something about it. Though for the life of her she didn't see what they could do.

Peter had a group around him in hectic discussion. When

she came in they glanced at her sharply, and Doris Matthews giggled. But Peter said something and they put their heads even closer together. Talking about her, were they? That did it.

Shortly afterward, Peter called the meeting to order. There was excitement in the air, but Peter managed to keep things under control.

"The Board of Education," he said, "has turned thumbs down on our proposal to start a Teen Club. It's really Mr. Leveridge, of course. He thinks it's nonsense, that there's no need for it here. We know there is. But we're up against a stone wall until we can convince him. The whole point of this meeting is, how are we going to do it?"

That set off a whirlpool of talk. The place seethed with it. Finally George Jenkins stood up.

"Why don't we forget it, then?" he asked in his lazy voice. "We've got enough to buck these days without bucking the stone wall, too. I guess we can get along."

Sally sprang to her feet. "That's ridiculous!" she cried. "We haven't even tried to get what we want—and need! Let's *do* something."

"Such as what?" Doris Matthews asked with a funny grin.

"Such as going to see Mr. Leveridge and telling him straight what we're after and why." She heard the words after she had said them, and was aghast. Suddenly, she knew what was coming.

"OK, let's put Sally on the job. She's yearning for trouble, and she's got enough temper to serve for a whole committee."

George made the suggestion just a little too patly, a little too quickly. She saw now what it was—a put-up job. That's what they had been talking about in the corner when she came in. They had decided that if she so much as opened her mouth, they'd give her the dirty work.

They thought they had her on the spot. Color flared in her cheeks, and her eyes shot sparks. She stood up, facing them.

"All right, I'll do it for the rest of you—sissies. Maybe you won't think it's so funny next week."

With that she sailed out of the room. There was an electric silence, and she had the brief satisfaction of knowing that her acceptance had stupefied them. It was Peter's doing. He wanted to take her down a couple of pegs. He was getting even for her display of temper toward him this morning. It was small, it was mean of him! She had never been so angry in her life.

"What's Mr. Leveridge like, Daddy?" she asked that night as they sat down to dinner.

She'd had time to think about what lay ahead of her, and she was pale with trepidation. She'd bitten off more than she could chew, and would the gang laugh when she choked on the wad they'd given her!

"Leveridge? Oh, he's short and wears glasses and has a red face . . ."

"I don't mean that way," Sally explained. "I mean—really."

"Peppery old duck. Has a temper like a shotgun. Goes off if you look sideways at him." He gave her a quick, amused glance. "Something like you. Why the interest in Leveridge?"

"He's head of the School Board," Sally said, above the lump in her throat. "And I'm going to see him."

Her father looked dazed. "Is that your idea of fun?"

"No," Sally said with a little more spirit, "it's the gang's."

And that was all she would tell him. Much as she would have liked to confide in someone, to feel her father's support and sympathy, she was afraid that if she began talking about it, she'd break down and give up. She *had* to go through with it.

And she did. Mr. Leveridge sat behind a massive walnut

desk that almost dwarfed him. He was just as Daddy had said, she noted with interest—short, red-faced, eyeglasses.

"Sit down, young lady," he boomed. He did not rise, and scarcely glanced at her. "You're wasting your time, I can tell you right now."

"Do you know what I've come for?" Sally asked.

"Generally speaking, yes. Some selfish plan of a particular little group. I don't know which group you represent, but all groups are alike—their own interests before anyone else's, and the devil take the hindmost."

Sally felt her temper rising—she knew the telltale signs—her nostrils flaring, the quick indrawn breath, a rush of words clamoring to be said. She pressed her lips together to keep the angry words from pouring out.

"That's not very fair of you, Mr. Leveridge," she managed at last, "to condemn us before we speak."

"Oh, it's not, isn't it?" he said belligerently. "Well, what's *your* particular gripe?"

He had no right to talk to her like that! She wanted to lash out, stingingly. A red mist was rising in front of her eyes.

"I'm not griping," she returned. Her jaw muscles ached with the effort she was making. "I represent the Juniors at Meadville High. And we're planning a Teen Club. We need your consent."

"Then you can take yourself off at once," he retorted. "Because I've already said I wouldn't give it."

"Are you the whole Board of Education?" That was daring, but she couldn't help it; it was out before she knew it.

"I'm the president of it," he said. "And what I say *goes*."

Hang on to yourself, Sally thought desperately. If you let go now, you're lost. He's being childish. I won't let him see how mad he's making me. She lifted her head and looked at him levelly.

"How can you decide whether or not we should have a Teen Club before you have even heard of our reasons?" she demanded.

His face grew redder, his eyes blazed behind the glasses. He pounded the desk with his fist, and his neck swelled visibly under his collar. If he could only see what he looks like, Sally decided with swift scorn. He's making a spectacle of himself with his temper. A sudden thought struck her. Glory! Was that the way she seemed to other people? She blushed with shame at the very thought—it was awful.

"Young lady," he bellowed, "no impertinence! I know why you youngsters want a Teen Club—because some other school has one, and you want to be equal to or ahead of them. Because you want to dance and stay out nights, instead of staying at home studying your lessons. Because you want a place to raise the roof with high jinks, and . . ."

This was too much! Sally leaned across the desk, tense and determined, calling on all her self-control as she had never called on it before. There was such a lot at stake. "Mr. Leveridge, that simply isn't so!" Her voice vibrated, and she could feel the blood pounding in her temples. This was important, and if she exploded now it would be all over. Mr. Leveridge was being ridiculous, but this time *she* wasn't going to be.

Still leaning across the desk she gave him the whole picture in short, snappy sentences. The trouble they had been having with the Meadville boys and girls who had no place to go for relaxation and pleasure, and the complaints of the overworked police department. She spoke of the success of other clubs, the enthusiasm already shown for them by the Chamber of Commerce and the Parent-Teachers and the Y's, and how they had promised to help with the project if the School Board would cooperate on it. Sally knew her stuff and she gave it to Mr. Leveridge with fire in her eyes and confidence in her voice. This was bigger than herself; this was for Meadville High and, more than that, for Meadville itself. He *had* to see it—it was up to her to make him see it.

She talked for ten minutes. Every time he mumbled an objection or grunted disbelief, she shot back with ready argument.

"If you want to know more, I'll be back tomorrow," she said. "If you want to talk to the others, I'll get them down here. But we've got to have that club, and we'll be around here until we get it."

Sally paused, out of breath. She had done her best, but her words had only made him more furious. He glared at her in an ominous, mounting silence. Suddenly he stood up and made a shooing movement with his hands.

"Get out!" he bellowed. "Get out—you've worn me down, can't you see? I've got other work to do."

"When's the next meeting of the Board?" Sally asked.

"Friday night," he replied.

"Then may we begin planning next week?"

"Get out of here!" he shouted. And when she still stood there, he added, "Young lady, I'd advise you to take up law."

She knew she'd won then. She smiled and held out her hand. "Thank you, Mr. Leveridge. That's the nicest compliment I ever had."

She didn't realize how tense she'd been until she was out of the office and down the street. Then she thought her knees would buckle under her. But she'd won. She'd shown the gang. . . . And then she stopped short. She had started out to show the gang, but she had shown herself something, too. It was quite a discovery. She had won because Mr. Leveridge had lost his temper and she had managed to keep hers. A temper was a grand thing to have—if you made it work for you. She'd have to tell Peter.

Suddenly it came to her. Maybe Peter knew that. Maybe that was why he'd forced her into this, so she'd find it out for herself.

"Do you want that apology now—or later?" Peter said, when she told him what had happened.

"I don't want one at all, Peter," she said.

She liked the way he was looking at her. For the first time, she was quite sure she knew how to keep him looking at her this way—from now on.

# Love Story

HELEN CIANCIMINO

# *Love Story*

Cathy Johanson hugged her knees hard as she swayed gently back and forth on the flat rock that the early spring sun had warmed. At her feet, the brook swirled and eddied, sparkling at a stray sunbeam that danced across its surface. The sunbeam caught in Lars Berglund's hair, too, and Cathy smiled down at his long figure lazily stretched on the green slope.

"You've got lashes like a girl's," Cathy informed him.

"When you start talking like that, it's time for me to leave." With mock dignity, Lars stood up.

Mixed with all the other emotions that filled Cathy's heart was a fierce pride in his bigness and his strength. From the direction of the Berglund farm someone was shouting his name and Lars grimaced.

"See you tomorrow," he promised.

He leaned over to hand her a bunch of long-stemmed violets. Then his lips brushed hers lightly. He turned and swung easily across the brook that separated the Berglund farm from the Johansons'.

Just for a moment, Cathy waited at the edge of the brook until the apple orchard hid him from view. Reluctantly she stood up and turned toward home. A fat robin winged swiftly off at her approach and a blue jay scolded at her from a tree. Once, lost in dreams, Cathy paused to hold the lovely blossoms against her cheek.

She was reliving that day only a few weeks before when she and Lars had laughed together over the antics of a newborn lamb and suddenly their eyes had met and she had really seen Lars for the first time. It was funny how all your life you took someone for granted, almost like an older brother, and then one day you noticed how his fair hair curled, how his shoulders were broad and muscular, and how his blue eyes on yours were filled with a special light.

"Have you really grown up, Cathy?" Lars had said that day as they bent over the ridiculous lamb that fell over its own clumsy feet. "I thought you never would!"

Just the memory of his words made Cathy's heart beat faster. This was different from anything she had felt before, from any of the crushes she had suffered through in other years. It was a magic world because she was in love and because it was spring.

I'm like that willow, Cathy's fancy ran as she rounded the corner of the house. Like me, it was plain and brown until spring touched it to that lovely pale green.

But the moment she stepped into the kitchen the spell was broken and everyday things caught up with her. The smell of baking bread, her mother's face reddened from bending over the oven, her brother John scrubbing his hands at the sink.

"Cathy, where have you been?" Tiredly, Mrs. Johanson pushed back a lock of hair. "The chickens to be fed, supper to get ready. What's come over you, child?"

Cathy stiffened. Wouldn't her mother ever understand that at sixteen you had long since passed childhood?

"Cathy's in love, Ma," John teased. "How can she bother with chores?"

"Love, indeed!" With a scornful thump Mrs. Johanson set a pan of potatoes before Cathy. "What do you know of love?"

Suddenly angry at John for his clumsy humor and at her mother for not even trying to understand, Cathy defended herself heatedly. "I know a lot!"

"And just what is it you know?" John taunted good-naturedly.

"I know it's beautiful and fine and . . ." Cathy's voice trailed off in embarrassment. She peeled potatoes furiously, conscious of John's grin and of her mother's intent look.

"Cathy, this Lars business has become too serious." Mrs. Johanson sounded troubled. "Maybe you'd better stop seeing him."

The knife clattered to the floor and Cathy stared unbelievingly at her mother. Not see Lars! You might as well try to stop the advance of spring as try to stop her from seeing Lars.

Words of protest crowded to Cathy's lips, but she checked them, hurt at the realization that already her mother's attention had wandered. Mrs. Johanson's gaze was fixed on the window through which one could see the barn with its coat of fresh paint that made the house seem shabbier by contrast and, in the field beyond, Mr. Johanson's figure silhouetted against the late afternoon sun.

"I told Pa I'd plough that field," John muttered.

"You can do other things," Mrs. Johanson answered absentmindedly, turning back to the oven to pull out the golden loaves of bread.

Cathy concentrated on the potatoes. The joy of the day was replaced by an aching sadness. Her mother was kind and good, but why couldn't she see past a pan of potatoes? The question held her. There must be a reason. Probably it was because Ma had never known this kind of love. There was Pa, of course, but Cathy almost smiled at the idea of Pa ever being romantic.

Something akin to pity filled Cathy as she watched her mother's busy progress around the kitchen. How could anyone understand magic who had never experienced it? And what must it be like to live your whole life without ever knowing the richness of the feeling that she and Lars shared?

Some of the pity was still with Cathy the next morning when she started for school. But her mind busied itself with the practical problem of what to do about Lars. The Berglunds were their only close neighbors, so it would be impossible not to see him at all. Surely her mother realized that!

The Red Oaks schoolhouse was a two-room brick building, but it had only one teacher. In the morning Cathy was a student, but in the afternoons she took charge of the lower grades. For the first time since she had been chosen to help with the younger children, they seemed noisy and tiresome and the day dragged to an end. Cathy delayed purposely till the school bus left, loaded with laughing girls and boys. She erased the blackboard, clapped the chalk dust from the erasers, and found a dozen tasks to keep her busy until the teacher left, too. Quickly, then, Cathy banked the coal stove and set the latch on the outer door. By cutting across the fields and through the orchards, she could reach the north pasture where Lars would be working today. Lars would find the right solution. He always knew what to do.

Not until she turned from the door did Cathy see the long car parked in the dusty road. Shining and sleek, it was unlike any that belonged in Red Oaks. The woman behind the wheel stared as Cathy approached, and all at once Cathy felt shy and countrified.

"Can I help you?" Cathy almost stammered, embarrassed because of the way the woman watched her.

"I thought . . . For a moment I thought you were someone else," the woman said with a little laugh, and shook her head the way you do when you've been daydreaming and someone brings you sharply back to reality. "It was twenty-five years ago, but . . ." Again the little shake of her head. "You look enough like Catherine Peters to be her twin!"

"I'm her daughter," Cathy volunteered shyly, unable to take her eyes off the smart suit the woman wore.

Now the woman's smile was cordial. "I'm Clara Winthrop," she introduced herself. "Red Oaks was my first teaching job and I couldn't resist a look at my past." Impulsively she opened the car door. "Won't you let me drive you home? I'd love to see your mother again."

Cathy had never ridden in anything as handsome as the roadster. With mounting excitement she sank back against its cushions. Strangers in Red Oaks were rare—especially such strangers. It would be worth waiting to see Lars to have such wonderful news to tell him!

A feeling of importance grew in her as she directed Miss Winthrop to the farm. After that it was like a holiday. Mrs. Johanson insisted that their guest stay for dinner and Cathy took pains to set the table with extra care. Mr. Johanson wore a jacket to the table and even John plastered his hair.

"It's like turning back the calendar twenty-five years," Mrs. Johanson said gaily.

All through dinner, that's what they did—turn back the calendar. Wide-eyed, Cathy listened to the refrain, "Do you remember . . . ?" Red Oaks had had a one-room schoolhouse then. Miss Winthrop had been the first teacher to come from the city. There had been no school bus, and she used to collect pupils in a Model T Ford. There had been a calf-lifting contest that Pa had won!

"Did you know Pa, too?" Cathy asked wonderingly.

"Know him! Why, he was the handsomest boy in Red Oaks, and every girl for miles around tried to make up to him." Miss Winthrop's chuckle was warm and throaty. "But he had eyes only for Catherine Peters. Every morning she found a note from him in the old oak tree. And the serenades he played on his harmonica under her window! I've never seen two people more in love."

Slowly Cathy looked from her mother to her father. Pa was stout and baldish. Ma looked older than Miss Winthrop. Yet once Pa had been like Lars—slim and handsome. And once Ma's hair had been as brown as Cathy's. And they really had been in love—the way she and Lars were. Cathy felt stunned. Was this what happened to the magic when spring was past?

"What was the prize for lifting the calf?" John was asking practically.

Cathy saw the long look that passed between her mother and her father. It was Pa who answered, but he seemed to be talking more to Ma than to John.

"The field just past the barn was the prize," he said quietly.

"Your mother was the real prize, John," Miss Winthrop protested. "Her parents wouldn't let her think of marrying unless your father owned some land of his own. You see, they were very young."

"I was just sixteen," Mrs. Johanson said softly. "Only Cathy's age . . ." Startled, her eyes met Cathy's, and Cathy couldn't face the tenderness in them. "Why, Cathy," her mother said gently, "I didn't realize how much I'd forgotten about being sixteen."

"How about dessert?" John demanded. Cathy wanted to hug him for being so unromantic as to change the subject. She couldn't bear her mother's understanding. Not now—not when she had herself just begun to understand. There had been magic in that spring so long ago. But now—she couldn't bear to think that magic could fade. What a trap love was!

Later, as she stood over a pan of soapy water, Cathy was doubly glad of the impulse that had led her to volunteer to straighten up the kitchen. She couldn't remember when she had seen Ma and Pa so relaxed, and she hated to have their mood interrupted. But that wasn't her only reason, she reflected honestly, as she polished each dish. She needed to be alone, to sort out all the conflicting emotions that she was experiencing.

Cathy sighed as she tackled the pots and pans almost viciously. How much easier it had been to believe that Ma had never known real love! Maybe it was silly to worry about how things would be in twenty-five years—why, that was practically forever!

Ma and Pa and Miss Winthrop were still sitting around the table when Cathy had finished cleaning up the dishes. Cathy dreaded the idea of having to listen to them any longer and she hovered uncertainly in the doorway, wondering how she could escape without being rude.

"Want to come over to the Berglunds' with me?" John asked. Mrs. Johanson smiled encouragingly, but Cathy shook her head.

"I have some studying to do, if you'll excuse me," she pleaded lamely.

Up in her room, she opened a textbook, but for all that she saw, its pages might have been blank. When she heard John go whistling up the road, she longed to shout, "Wait for me!" The Berglunds would have a fire lighted and Lars would play records and they would dance. At the thought of Lars, a tear slid down Cathy's cheek. Lars had waited for her to grow up. Lars loved her . . . But did Lars understand about love?

Restlessly, Cathy prowled around the little attic that Lars and John had helped her make over into a room. Once she caught a glimpse of herself in the mirror and she was re-assured by her tall, slim reflection, by the cascade of hair, shining and richly brown. She knelt at the window and looked out into the spring night and sniffed the flower-scented air. Down on the porch she could hear voices. Ma and Pa emerged, walking Miss Winthrop to the gate.

"The sky in the city is a poor thing compared to this!" Miss Winthrop sounded wistful. Her voice was even more wistful when she added, "And it's been wonderful seeing you two together sharing such a full life."

Their good-bys were a jumble, and then the long car disappeared into the night. Ma and Pa stood a moment at the gate in silence. Cathy saw that their faces were lifted contentedly to the sky. Without a word, they walked slowly into the house, but Cathy found herself leaning far out of the window to watch them. Maybe it was the spring night, but in the shadows they walked close together, like young lovers! Suddenly Cathy felt peaceful and secure—and sleepy.

Sunlight streamed into the room and the birds outside competed loudly in their own symphony of spring. Cathy smiled drowsily over the familiar noises that drifted up to the attic. John's rooster crowed. The chickens clucked and fussed. The pigeons cooed. Cathy dressed swiftly, but John was the only one left at the breakfast table and he was absorbed in a farm journal propped against the sugar bowl.

Without looking up, he mumbled to Cathy, "Lars is driving to town this morning. He'll give you a lift to school."

Cathy almost spilled the glass of milk she was holding. Once a week the trip to town had to be made to transact both the Berglunds' and the Johansons' business and for years John and Lars had alternated, but this was John's week! John was always eager for an opportunity to spend the day in town . . . A horn honked insistently.

"Well, what are you waiting for? That's Lars," John said gruffly.

Cathy picked up her books and ran. Lars had the car door open, and his smile was as dazzling as the morning itself. Looking at him. Cathy felt joyous. It was wonderful to ride beside him. The car was an old rattletrap, but she was riding with Lars and she wouldn't change for six of Miss Winthrop's low-slung roadsters that purred.

"I missed you yesterday," Lars said.

Yesterday was a long day, Cathy thought. All the confused impressions in her mind were falling into a pattern. John teasing her, but giving up his trip to town so that she could ride with Lars. Miss Winthrop remembering Ma and Pa when they were first in love, and still envying them their "full" life. Pa, unromantic and thick-waisted, but still working the field that had made it possible for him to marry Ma. And Ma—only yesterday, Cathy remembered, she had thought that Ma couldn't see past a pan of potatoes, because Ma had said Cathy didn't know what love was.

"I didn't understand," Cathy whispered.

"Why didn't you come over with John last night?" Lars was asking.

Cathy hesitated, and then the words came in a rush. "I was finding out that a pan of potatoes are as much a part of love as the violets you gave me yesterday!" Stumblingly she told him all her discoveries, but the words came more easily as she saw the smile that lighted Lars's face.

"Cathy, Cathy, you've really grown up!" For a second he took his hand from the wheel to hold hers, and they sat in silence.

Cathy stole a sidelong glance at Lars who was whistling tunelessly. "Lars," she said shyly, "if you had to do one thing to show your love for me, what would it be?"

Cathy stole a sidelong glance at Lars, who was whistling a long while before he said gravely, "I guess there's no answer to that, Cathy. Except—everything. If you look, you'll see it every day, as long as you live, in everything I do."

# Lady, You Started Something

MARGUERITE EYSSEN

# Lady, You Started Something

Laura was frosting a chocolate cake hopefully, because Deedie still found food very consoling. She made the frosting especially thick this time and sighed for the days when Emma Brandon had been sufficient unto any family crisis. If the children came down with the measles, if Laura were blinded by a sick headache, if company were coming and the guest room a shambles, she'd simply call Emma and that was all there was to it. Widowed, and with a son of her own to support, Emma could turn her hand to anything and she did.

But Laura's crises had now outgrown Emma. Time had washed a good first mate overboard and the sailing was getting rough. Turk was sixteen now and Deedie was going on fifteen. It had been all very well to call Emma once and say, "Emma, Turk's croup isn't any better, and I haven't slept for two nights—spell me off, can you?" or, "Emma, Deedie has a rash on her stomach and the doctor can't decide—come over, will you?" But she couldn't call Emma and say, "Emma, what on earth are we going to do about Turk's crush on Lucille Loring?" or "Emma, where in the world can I find some unwary adolescent with enough manners to ask Deedie to a high school dance?"

Looking up now, Laura saw Deedie standing in the kitchen doorway, carrying her books under her arm. She didn't so much as glance at the cake, though, or the frosting still clinging temptingly to bowl and spoon. Her face was hot and flushed with rushing home from school. Hope fought with young despair in her eyes.

"Anybody call for me, Mom?" she asked breathlessly, and Laura reflected that hope does indeed die hard. The Friday night dance in the gym was only a matter of three hours away.

"No, Deedie," she said gently. "How about a piece of cake?"

"No, thanks," said Deedie, turning away, and Laura heard her go slowly up the stairs. Darn these male adolescents, anyhow! thought Laura. I could wring their necks. The child was taking this thing harder every time; for Deedie to turn down anything either chocolate or sweet was unprecedented.

Presently Deedie came back into the kitchen. She had changed into her habitual khaki jodhpurs, topped by an old sweater with the sleeves pushed above her elbows. Sometimes when Deedie got out of her pleated skirt, as she invariably did the minute she reached home, Laura could hardly tell at first glance whether it was Deedie or Turk. Boyishly slim and agile, Deedie had grown up in trousers. Now she swung herself up onto the sink, sat there forlornly swinging her feet. Someday, thought Laura, looking at the fine line of her eyebrows, the full, sweet mouth, Deedie was going to be pretty, very pretty indeed.

"Might as well get going on the lawn, I guess," her daughter said dully. "Nobody's going to call now." She usually clipped the edges of the lawn while Turk did the mowing. Turk was her idol and, as yet, the dominant influence in her life. Her desire to be with Turk, to do as Turk did, still shaped all Deedie's ends. From the time Deedie had been able to toddle after him, the most effective punishment Laura could devise had been to separate her from Turk, in spite of the fact that Turk had learned early to drive hard bargains with her, to make her pay well for the fact that she was a girl, and younger.

"Wear gloves, Deedie," urged Laura, glancing at Deedie's roughened hands clasped around one knee.

"Can't work in gloves," she answered. "Turk doesn't wear gloves."

"But you're a girl, dear," reminded Laura, and Deedie's face clouded ominously.

"I hate being a girl!" she said. "Mom, I—I'd just as soon be dead as be a girl."

There it was! What to do about it, too, was more than Laura could figure out. If only one of the young barbarians who habitually overran her house would ask Deedie to go to the high school dances. But a stone wall would be more easily penetrated than their indifference. Beset, her heart aching for the child, she watched Deedie through the kitchen window clipping conscientiously around the tulip bed while Turk charged back and forth with the lawnmower. Turk finished first and sauntered into the kitchen, sat blithely down at the table with the frosting bowl and spoon.

"Turk," Laura asked him, "why is it none of the boys ever asks Deedie to go to the dances?"

Turk looked up from the bowl, his eyes popping. The thought was so astounding that the wooden spoon stopped halfway to his mouth.

"*Deedie!*" he said. "Dance?"

"Don't be dull!" Laura said crossly. "She's a freshman, isn't she? And all the other girls in her class go. Your friends seem to like the popcorn balls and fudge she makes for you, and you wouldn't go on a hike without her, any of you, because she cleans the skillets and washes the coffeepot. You prob-

ably let her build the fire, too, but when it comes to being
nice to her . . ."

"Gosh, Mom," said Turk, abashed, "I don't know."

He sat there, wrinkling his forehead, cannily giving it his
best thought, and Laura's resentment flared into anger.

"Oafs!" she said inclusively.

"Well, gosh!" complained Turk. "Can I help it? The fellows all think Deed's a good egg and all, but dance—heck,
Deed's not the type."

"Oh!" said Laura, her eyes narrowing. And then, "No?"

"Uh-huh," said Turk with callous finality. "There's just
something Deed hasn't got, that's all."

"Oh!" said Laura again. And then, "Yes?"

"Well," Turk said. "You asked me, didn't you? You wanted
to know, didn't you? And can I help it? What can I do about
it?"

"Begin by helping Deedie finish the lawn—and now, darling!" suggested Laura helpfully.

She saw Turk approach Deedie, take the clippers out of her
grasp with one hand, and, with the other, rumple Deedie's
dark curls roughly. Deedie retaliated by jerking his shirt tail
out and the battle was on, ending by Turk's rubbing her pert
nose in the turf until she shrieked, "Uncle! Uncle!" It was
typical, all right; but Laura had always regarded the way in
which Deedie had grown up with Turk and his friends as a
wholesome state of affairs. All boys were merely lesser editions
of Turk to Deedie and she was Turk's kid sister to them.
There was plenty of time, certainly, for Deedie to hold the
whip hand as she would indeed someday.

Plenty of time? Heavenly day, the girl, going on fifteen, was
already relegated to a merciless category: a good egg and all,
handy little squaw, but dance—heck, she wasn't the type. Why,
if I'd begun the day she was born with this boy-meets-girl

business, thought Laura worriedly, I'd still be too far behind the bandwagon. Then her common sense asserted itself.

Deedie was the ideal child for her age: clear-eyed, straightforward, generous. Older people invariably adored her, and younger children dogged her heels. Never yet had Deedie ever dared to presume upon her sex. She had had to compensate for it, rather, by popcorn balls and fudge and doing the more disagreeable chores. Laura had suffered this for Deedie on the ground that it was good training through these formative years for the time when, unless Laura missed her guess, Deedie would hold more than one heart in the hollow of her hand.

But it hadn't worked out any too well for Deedie. Even now, there was something dejected and forlorn in Deedie's outline as she sat there on the lawn, her hands clasped around her ankles, her chin on her knees, her eyes following Turk.

Turk was going to the dance, of course. He was taking Lucille Loring, and the bare thought of Lucille Loring brought on Laura's grimace of distaste. Lucille was indeed the dancing type—dancing was her natural métier. More than rhythm and music to Lucille, dancing was opportunity, and Laura had watched her flutter from partner to partner on the front porch while the radio blared, watched her a little grimly. Lucille was the kind of girl who swept the field at sixteen and was an old story at twenty.

Still, Laura looked up from her knitting at Turk and smiled when he came downstairs after dinner fairly glistening, every inch the privileged male aggressor. She might have to come to grips with him sooner or later about Lucille Loring, but in the meantime he was no problem. Greg, comfortably ensconced behind the evening paper with his pipe, glanced quizzically up at Turk. He waited until the door had slammed behind Turk and then he said, "Well, Lucille Loring certainly has something! I never thought Turk would actually learn to wash behind the ears." Laura's mouth tightened.

"I don't know what to do about Lucille," she said, and Greg chuckled.

"Why criticize success?" he asked.

"But she's just too—well, too . . ."

"Say it!" Greg dared her.

"Too great a reflection upon masculine insight," Laura said crisply, and Greg laughed outright.

"There's no such thing as masculine insight at sixteen," he told her. "Something will just have to hit Turk between the eyes, eventually."

Putting aside her knitting, Laura went upstairs to tap on Deedie's door. Deedie's room was a faithful duplicate of Turk's. There was the same single bed with its plain durable spread. Deedie's skis, like Turk's, were decoratively crossed on the wall. Deedie lay flat on her stomach on the bed, her head buried in the pillow. She rolled over and sat up, swallowing, as Laura came in. But she hadn't been crying. Stiff and aching as the muscles of her face might be from rigid control, Deedie wouldn't cry; tears had never got her anywhere with Turk.

"Don't you care, Deedie," begged Laura. "There'll be other dances. Lots of them, dear, and someday . . ."

"No," Deedie said with despairing conviction. "Not for me, anyhow. There's something wrong with me, Mom. I—I'm just different, that's all. Everybody and her dog got a bid. Everybody but—but me."

"There's not one single thing wrong with you," Laura argued. "Why, the idea, Deedie! You're just as sweet and pretty as you can be and someday . . ."

Deedie's eyes, full of young wretchedness, turned to Laura's.

"Everybody's pretty to—to her mother, I guess," she said.

Laura was silent, holding Deedie's rough little hand in hers, torn between two mental images: the image of Lucille Loring, unbelievably precocious and knowing at sixteen and the image of Deedie saying, "There's something wrong with me, Mom." Why, how many times had the quick turn of Deedie's head, the nice eyebrows like wings in flight, the sheen of the wavy mop in the sun, suggested to Laura that she must have been prescient when she'd called her daughter Diana. She must have known even then that Deedie would be slender and lithe and lovely someday. Someday, yes. But what about now? Laura thought of the way Lucille Loring managed her eyelashes, and she shivered.

Downstairs, Greg, comfortable and unconcerned, still read his paper and puffed at his pipe. Laura, two harried little lines between her eyes, sat down again with her knitting.

"You know Deedie wanted to go to the dance, too," she said. "But—but nobody asked her."

Greg looked up from his paper and his jaw dropped.

"Deedie!" he said. "Dance?"

Laura's mouth tightened again. The child's own father.

"The worst of it is," she said, "she's getting the idea that she's different."

"Well, she is different—thank heaven!" said Greg fervently, and Laura, her eyes flashing, said, "Greg, you're impossible!"

"Why, what have I said now?" demanded Greg, for all the world like Turk, and Laura said, "The child is actually suffering, Greg."

Greg laid his paper aside then, pondering as he refilled his pipe. Deedie was his heartstring.

"I'll take her with me to Canada on a fishing trip this summer," he decided finally, and Laura raked him with a glance.

"Fishing!" she said. "When she wants to dance?"

"She won't have the right bait for that," Greg warned her. "Not for about five years."

It *was* easier said than done, of course. Laura could begin by prodding Deedie about her hands, her hair, the eternal jodhpurs, but to be successful, the stimulus should come from within the girl herself. What Deedie needed was to find herself pretty in somebody's eyes besides her mother's, and soon. If only somebody would ask her to a high school dance! Laura could, she supposed, speak to some of her friends who were mothers of boys, but she knew too well what Turk would do in a similar situation. Even if he yielded in the end, he'd ooze martyrdom from every pore.

She woke in the morning, still perturbed, to admit Emma Brandon. They had decided to clean Greg's clothespress that day. Pink-cheeked and gray-haired and imperturbable, Emma took one look at her and said, "Who's sick, Mrs. Dallow?"

"Nobody, Emma. I couldn't get to sleep last night, that's all."

Emma stood rolling up her sleeves as Laura laid out Greg's tweed suit, frowning thoughtfully. It was a handsome suit but it had never really fitted Greg and he would, of course, wear it as long as it hung there. Besides, Emma's son Bill was graduating this year and the suit was navy blue.

"Here, Emma, you take this," she said with sudden decision. "It should be just right for Bill."

All Emma's maternal instinct was in her eyes as she looked at the suit. She said, "It's so much nicer than anything he could buy. Although he—he hasn't had to buy any clothes for two years." Laura smothered a smile. It was one of Greg's stock quips that the only thing that kept him covered was the fact that some of his clothes were too sober in color and cut for Bill Brandon.

"Think of the honor and distinction for me, Emma," Laura

said now. "After all, look who Bill is! Heavens, when I think of the girl trouble you must have!"

"Girls!" Emma said, successfully sidetracked. "Thank goodness, Bill doesn't have the time or the money. He works in Waring's shoe store after school and Saturdays; but while he's there all *I* do is answer the telephone."

"Nothing ventured, nothing won!" laughed Laura. "And I know how these young girls feel, Emma. Why, I'd give my heart, almost, if one of the boys in Deedie's class would ask her to a high school dance."

"Bill would ask her," Emma said, and Laura laughed again.

"Have you no sense of proportion, Emma?" she said. "Why, Bill's a senior and the football captain, and Deedie's only Turk's kid sister. What I'm looking for is some unwary young fly who will walk into my parlor and never know the difference."

"There aren't any," Emma told her. "But you can't sell shoes to women without manners, and Bill does very well at that."

"Emma," Laura said, horrified, "if you think I would put Bill in a spot . . ."

"*I* would," Emma said.

"You mean you'd *try* to," said Laura, "and thanks just the same. Do we have to hang all these things out?"

The school dances were mercifully only monthly affairs but, even so, Laura was beginning to regard them as the bane of her existence and the school's error. They put a premium on the Lucille Loring brand of charm and made life unendurable for girls like Deedie, and for their mothers. Laura had all she could do to contain herself the day she met one of Deedie's teachers, and Miss Smithers said, "They're bound to dance somewhere, you know, and we'd rather it would be at the school." Laura reflected how much teachers didn't know. Just how was Deedie going to dance, anywhere?

It was that same day that she answered the telephone to hear a young male voice say, "Is Deedie there? No, thank you, I'll call again." If he hadn't said thank you; if he'd merely said OK and hung up, she'd have dismissed the call from her mind as a probable usual request to borrow Deedie's racket or fishing tackle. As it was, though, she said to Deedie, as they were getting dinner, "Some boy called you, Deedie."

She saw the pulse begin to pound in the little hollow at the base of Deedie's throat. "Who—who was it?" she asked breathlessly.

"He didn't say, dear."

"You mean you—you let him get away?" Deedie wailed.

"Deedie, for heaven's sake! He said he'd call again."

Deedie stood taut, thinking, and then the pulse slowed down.

"It was Butch," she decided dismally. "He'll call again. He wants me to trade rackets with his sister Lorna, and I don't want to."

The telephone rang again, and Laura caught Deedie's hand as she started for it. "Deedie," she said. "Don't trade rackets if you don't want to. Why should you?"

"Oh, I know," mourned Deedie. "But Lorna's really is too light for her, and I could use it, and mine is heavier. It—it seems kind of mean not to."

Stricken, Laura took Deedie's face between her hands and kissed her. "Deedie," she said, "your life is richer than any other girl's, really. We measure it, you know, by the number of people we love—not by the ones who love us."

"All right," said Deedie dully. "I'll trade. I—I don't care."

She looked dazed when she came back to the kitchen, as if she were walking in a dream. Her eyes were wide and blank.

"It—was—Bill Brandon," she said in a monotone. "It was! He asked me to go to the dance."

"Oh!" gasped Laura, and then, "W-e-ll!"

"You don't know who he is," shrilled Deedie as her voice rose in hysterical crescendo. "He's a senior and he's the team captain and he's . . . Pinch me. No, don't. I—I don't want to wake up."

"Deedie, stop it!" scolded Laura, shaking her. "Stop it this minute!"

Deedie's head went down on her shoulder, and torn with rending sobs, Deedie clung to her. Frightened now, Laura sensed something of Deedie's yearning to be like other girls, the depth of her grief over being different. But she decided she had been right in trying to keep Deedie her age. She was too young, too emotionally unbalanced for this sort of thing. Then Deedie's head came up. She dried her eyes. "I wish," she sniffed, "I had a dress just like—like Lucille Loring's!"

"I'll take care of it, Deedie," promised Laura with more valor than discretion.

For it dawned upon her, as she made the rounds of dress shops that for fifteen-year-old girls the shops sponsored only two schools of thought: the bag-tied-in-the-middle school, specializing in wide white sashes, and the Lucille Loring school, letting the chips fall where they would. It wasn't until toward the end of the day that, tired and dispirited, she happened upon a dress that looked as if some inspired designer had said to herself mischievously, "Fifteen? Hmmmmmmm—fifteen!" The corners of Laura's mouth twitched as the saleswoman held up the dress, so delicious, so tempting. Mentally Laura was already slipping it over Deedie's head. But Deedie was so young, so unformed. If she could just keep her a child for one more year, even six months. And then again she heard Turk saying with callous finality, "There's just something Deedie hasn't got, that's all."

"Send it!" she said.

She had to stand over Deedie Friday night, as Deedie nervously pulled on the gossamer stockings. Deedie's eyes were wide and dark, their pupils distended. Her hands were icy cold. Tiny beads of sweat stood out on her upper lip, her forehead. Her fingers shook as she fumbled with the straps of the fragile sandals. "Here, let me do it," Laura said finally. The long pink slip fitted Deedie like her skin, just grazing the floor. Her wavy mop had been brushed until it shone in the light. Laura slipped the dress over Deedie's head and stood back to view it judicially.

It was organdy; dusty pink. Cunningly it followed the lines of Deedie's lithe slenderness as far as her knees where it flared out suddenly in a wide swirl to the floor. The high round neck was deceptively demure and the sleeves were brief, transparent puffs. Laura's throat tightened as she looked at her child, and her own fingers shook when she pinned the bright blue butterfly in the dark hair. Deedie's eyes clung to hers, anxiously probing, until Laura took her firmly by the hand to lead her across the hall to the long mirror in the guest room.

"Deedie, dear," she smiled uncertainly and waved to the mirror in an airy effort to break the tension, "this is Miss Diana Dallow!"

Deedie caught her breath sharply. She walked slowly toward the mirror and laid the flat of her hands against it, her eyes widening. Then, as the doorbell pealed through the house, panic gripped her, and she put her hands to her face, trembling. "Mom," she said, "I—I'm scared. Oh, tell him—tell him I'm sick."

For a minute, Laura wavered; and then she thought of all Emma Brandon must have gone through to achieve this.

"Deedie, this is the same Bill Brandon who used to pull you

on your sled, remember? Look in the mirror, dear. Stand right there and look until I call you."

Downstairs, something of Deedie's panic seized Laura as Bill rose from his chair. He was—was simply super, of course. Tall and broad of shoulder, he looked like a blond Norse god but something about his fixed smile, the very faultlessness of his approach betrayed the connivance which had brought him here. There was nothing for it now, though, but to stand at the foot of the stairs and call, "Deedie, Bill's here."

The door of the guest room opened and Laura held her breath. But as Deedie floated down the stairs on the crest of the pink swirl, her chin came up, and Laura caught again that quick turn of the small head. Greg was standing in front of the mantel filling his pipe. Glancing up to see Deedie on the landing, he held the tobacco pouch in midair, the tobacco spilling over onto the hearth as he stared at Deedie, blinking.

"Hello, Bill," said Deedie shyly, coming on down, and all of a sudden Bill's fixed smile faded as he stared, too.

"Gosh, Deedie!" he muffed it, reddening. "Why . . . hello."

When the door had closed behind them, Laura dropped limply into a chair and said to Greg, "Well, that's over!"

"Over!" said Greg, sweeping up tobacco with the hearth brush. "It's just begun. You've started something, lady!"

Yes, they had started something, she and Emma. Laura knitted doggedly at a scarlet sweater for Deedie after Greg had gone to bed, her eyes turning every fifteen minutes to the clock. She could hardly follow the pattern for alternating between seeing Deedie fluttering from partner to partner and seeing that fixed smile again on Bill's face as he was stuck with Deedie, her eager little face turning white and wretched.

By some miracle, Turk reached home first. He came in and

slumped down into a corner of the sofa, looking as if he'd been anesthetized and hadn't come out of it.

"Deedie stopped the show," he said, as if he were talking to himself. "And Bill Brandon—gosh! How did she snag that cagey bird unless—unless you asked his mother?"

"I'll tell you a secret," she said pleasantly. "But don't let it get any further than Lucille, will you, Turk? Bill's mother asked *me!*"

Illogically, Laura's heart sank as Deedie came down late to Saturday breakfast. Gone were the disreputable jodhpurs, the sweater with rolled-up sleeves, the sneakers. Deedie came trailing the folds of the taffeta housecoat her Aunt Sarah had given her for Christmas, teetering on the absurd mules to match. Just last Christmas she hadn't been able to see Sarah's gift for the skis exactly like Turk's, and ever since the housecoat had lain forgotten in its tissue paper. The blended scents of her own bath powder and hand cream assailed Laura in full force, indicating real zeal. The crowning effect was the bright blue butterfly again perched in Deedie's hair, this time with an air of permanence.

"Latest thing for clipping lawns?" Turk inquired caustically.

Before Deedie could retort, the telephone rang and Turk went to answer it since all the Saturday morning calls were for him. He came back to stand in the archway, a high flush spreading across his cheekbones.

"It's Butch," he told Deedie. "He says for Lucille and me and—and you to come along to the first show tonight."

"No, thanks," said Deedie. But Deedie loved movies! Turk's chin shot forward.

"Just because you don't like Lucille," he began and stopped as Deedie looked up at him.

"Remember, I didn't say anything to Lucille, Turk," Deedie said. "She—she said it to me."

Turk went back to the telephone, and Laura said, "What did Lucille say, Deedie?"

"We were all at the same table in the dogwagon afterward," Deedie told her. "And Lucille said to Bill that she knew he sold shoes after school and Saturdays, but she hadn't known he worked nights, too, until—until now."

"Deedie! And don't tell me Turk didn't . . ."

"He couldn't say anything, Mom. Lucille was his date. He just got red the way he does, you know. I didn't say anything because I couldn't think right away what she meant. But Butch got mad, and he said to her, 'Don't be a heel, just because you know how!' Then Trigger got mad, too. But Bill just laughed at Lucille."

Laura stared at Deedie, fascinated.

"What she meant, of course, Mom," said Deedie, emptying the sugar bowl on her cereal, "was that it was work for Bill to drag me, and his mother must have made him do it or something. But his mother didn't do any such thing. I asked him and Bill told me so."

"What!" gasped Laura.

"You see, Mom, Bill's on the dance committee, and the teachers wrote down all the names of girls that hadn't been to a dance this year, and then each one of the committee drew one, and Bill drew mine. Only don't tell Turk because it's a secret and I'm the only one who knows it except the committee."

Her elbows on the table, Laura rested her head in her hands. The telephone rang, and when she looked up, Turk stood in the archway again.

"It's Trigger," he told Deedie in a subdued voice. "He gets the car tonight and he wants me to go on a double date with you and him. Maybe—I might ask Maddy Maltby."

"No, thanks," said Deedie.

"S-a-y!" demanded Turk. "Who do you think you are?"

"Miss Diana Dallow," said Deedie.

"OK, duchess!" drawled Turk. "For all I care, you can sit here and wait for the duke to drop in."

"He didn't say he'd call," owned Deedie, "but I bet he will!"

Laura waited until the door had slammed behind Turk, then she said, "Aren't you expecting a lot of the committee, Deedie?"

"I didn't say the committee would call. I said I bet Bill would."

"But I'd be nice to all the boys and not too nice to just a special one, Deedie."

"Not if the one was Bill, you wouldn't!" Deedie said.

"Deedie, Bill has work to do. He doesn't have either the time or the money to . . ."

"But he doesn't need money," explained Deedie. "Why, it's simply super, Mom, all the colleges that want him, and Mr. Waring's already got him a job in a shoe store where one of them is. Besides, shoe stores close at nine o'clock on Saturdays."

She volunteered to dust the living room to be within one leap of the telephone. Making the beds upstairs, Laura left the doors open, listening, grimly ready to take charge. The next youngster who called was going to find himself high man. Bill Brandon certainly wasn't going to bother with little Deedie, and Laura was not going to let this thing begin all over again. She heard the telephone ring and dashed into the hall.

"Oh, hello, Bill," she heard Deedie say, and she dropped weakly down on the top step. Very obviously Bill was asking Deedie to go to the movies, the second show. So this was

Turk's cagey bird, this was Emma's son with neither the time nor the money . . . Emma couldn't be behind this, either.

"Deedie!" Laura called, and then she heard Deedie saying, "Let's skip the movies. It's going to be a nice night and I thought we'd all dance here. You—you could drop in."

Laura was silent as Deedie hung up and came to sit beside her on the top step. She couldn't have spoken to save her life.

"It was Bill," Deedie confided. "But it—it costs a lot to go to the movies, Mom. I'll make a cake or something and I'll ask Turk and Maddy Maltby, and Butch and Lorna, and Trigger and Lois, and . . ."

She stopped to catch her breath, and suddenly her arms went around Laura's neck in a convulsive squeeze.

"Oh, Mom," she whispered, "it—it's simply grand to be a girl."

Holding her close, Laura laid a damp cheek against Deedie's hair. Grand to be a girl? Far grander to be a girl's mother.

# Prairie Song

EDITH BISHOP SHERMAN

# Prairie Song

In the gaunt February landscape, that Saturday morning, the little farmhouse seemed to huddle like a solitary, frightened sheep beneath the lee of the hill. Carol Boyd, lifting the flapping curtain of the old station wagon, the better to see her home as it must appear to her guest, thought it would not have seemed quite so weather-beaten and lonely if her father could have used better paint when renovating it last summer. But always it was a question of expense, of making things do until better times, she remembered with dissatisfaction. Then, with Frank, the hired man, at the wheel, the station wagon rattled down over the prairie slope and into the farmyard.

"Well, we're here," said Carol rather inanely to the girl beside her. She tugged with stiff, cold fingers at the car door. "I should think Dad or you could have done something about this lock, Frank," she added impatiently.

"We will, soon's we get time," answered Frank, not offering to help with Hildegarde's suitcase.

Carol jerked the case out of the car and stalked toward the bare, windswept front porch, followed by her guest. When will Dad and Frank take time to mend anything around here if not now, in winter? she thought. In summer they never seemed to get ahead of the everlasting farm work, except when they worked at night, by lantern light, as Dad had in painting the house.

"Frozen?" she asked aloud of Hildegarde.

"Not exactly dying with the heat." The other laughed, trying to control her chattering teeth.

"You might have been warmer if the curtains on that station wagon hadn't been so full of holes, and hadn't flapped so in the wind," remarked Carol. She opened the door. "Now run through this arctic zone we call the front hall—there's a fire in the living-room stove."

At least the living room would be cozy and as neat as her broom and dustcloth could make it before she had driven into town with Frank to meet Hildegarde's train, she reflected. But her first hasty glance, as she crossed its threshold, told her that Timmy and his toys had changed its orderliness into turmoil.

"Timmy Boyd!" she began wrathfully, and stopped. Oh, what was the use? She just shouldn't have asked Hildegarde Horton to visit her, in spite of Mother's saying that she knew the daughter of her own old schoolmate would enjoy coming down to the farm. Although Mother had been entertained in the Hortons' luxurious home in Des Moines during the State Fair Week, with Timmy and Carol herself, she simply didn't realize what a shock it must be to Hildegarde to see how poor people like the Boyds had had to exist since moving out to farm country in Iowa. A swift vision rose before Carol of the other girl's spacious bedroom, of quiet, efficient servants picking up wraps, serving meals. What would Mrs. Horton say when her daughter told her that the Boyds ate in the kitchen because there was no dining room in the crowded little farm-house? She could imagine the expression which would settle upon Mrs. Horton's face when, home again, Hildegarde would describe her awful weekend visit. What difference did it make that Mrs. Horton had visited the Boyds' own lovely home back East, before they had lost everything in the depression? It was now that counted!

The next instant Carol's heart sank still lower for, in un-happy contrast to Hildegarde's smartly garbed, dignified mother, Mrs. Boyd appeared from the adjacent kitchen, her skirts pinned back, her hair flying untidily, and a soapy mop clutched in her water-reddened hands.

"Back so soon, dear? Why, I didn't expect you until dinner time!" exclaimed Mrs. Boyd, her tone aghast. She sent a swift glance toward the clock ticking upon its homemade shelf be-hind the big round stove.

Carol stiffened. Mother knew that Hildegarde had written about a choice of two trains, that there had been a possibility of her arriving on the earlier one. Why, then, wasn't she ready, dressed in the best she had? But before Carol could open her lips to answer, Mrs. Boyd had turned to welcome the newcomer.

"My dear, how happy we are to have you here," she said with cordiality.

"And how glad I am to be here!" responded Hildegarde, moving forward impulsively to kiss her.

A pang struck Carol as she gazed at her guest's slim, fur-coated figure. It would be easy to echo graciousness, to be poised and charming in clothes like those!

"Luncheon ready, Mother?" she inquired pointedly. Then, suddenly she became aware of an acrid odor of something burning. "What on earth is that terrible cindery smell? You get it as soon as you step inside!"

Mrs. Boyd laughed. "My cake for the church supper to-night! Burned to a crisp while I was telephoning to Mrs. Bennett about the supper. No," she interrupted herself to answer her daughter, "dinner isn't quite ready yet. That telephone call set me back in cleaning the kitchen, too." Her face clouded as her glance followed Carol's to the corner where, amid blocks and picture books, Hildegarde was kneeling to greet Timmy. "I'm sorry about his mussing up the living room after you had straightened it so nicely, dear," Mother added, her tone apologetic. "But I had to get the little fellow out of the kitchen so I could mop it, and it was warm in here for him."

"Couldn't he have taken his toys and played upstairs?" Carol asked, frowning.

Mrs. Boyd shook her head. "Too cold for him, after his bout with croup last week. No, this room was the only place for him, Carol."

"Oh, all right—only I did want at least one spot decent for Hildegarde in this horrid little house of ours," replied the girl under her breath.

As soon as she had said it she was sorry, for keen hurt showed a fleeting instant in her mother's eyes. Then Hildegarde, having made no headway with Timmy, rose to her feet.

"There's gratitude for you!" She chuckled. "I spent torturing hours dragging Timmy Boyd around the fairgrounds last summer, while my feet hurt, and now he won't even speak to me!" She struck an attitude of mock despair. "No, don't tell me it's bashfulness. It's just brutal indifference. Men are all alike!"

Carol joined in the laughter, but her depression was increased for now a tinge of remorse had been added to it as she remembered with what eagerness her mother had joined in her plans for this visit. Then Timmy's high treble broke into his sister's thoughts.

"I will so speak to you," he said to Hildegarde, peeping at her from behind chubby hands. "You buyed me ice-cream cones at the Fair. I'd like one now."

"Mercy, in weather like this?" remonstrated Hildegarde with a shiver.

"Oh, my dear, you're cold, aren't you?" said Mrs. Boyd at once. "Come on over to the stove! Better still, take her upstairs, Carol, and let her freshen up a bit while I hurry dinner. Warm food will be the thing!"

Freshen up! And dinner, instead of luncheon! Carol's lips curled. It was bad enough to have to live out here on the prairies, without Mother's lapsing into all the farm expressions.

Thoroughly ill-tempered by now, Carol had to make an effort to appear cheerful while Hildegarde unpacked her expensive little monogrammed bag and hung her dainty possessions away in the closet. And down in the big farm kitchen, Carol's depression returned threefold. Never had the place seemed so steamy and noisy. True, there was a clean white cloth on the table, and her mother had brought out her best china and silver. But there was a darned patch in the cloth at Hildegarde's chair, and the best china did not go with Frank's overalls, or with his red, good-natured face as he slid clumsily into his seat. His very presence at the table was a sore point with Carol. When she had asked that he be served separately, her mother had firmly refused.

"Why not?" the girl had persisted. "He's only a hired man, Mother."

"He's been your father's and my good friend ever since we came West," Mrs. Boyd had answered. "Neither of us knew anything about farm life, Carol. Besides, he is the nephew of a kind neighbor."

Now Carol flopped somewhat sullenly into her own chair while, in his courtly fashion, Mr. Boyd assisted Hildegarde to be seated and, small as he was, Timmy did the same for his mother.

Instead of the creamed chicken and hot biscuits that Mrs. Boyd had promised to serve, the meal was a hastily prepared one of salt pork, scrambled eggs, and warmed-over turnips, with crullers instead of delicious apple pie for dessert. It was horrid, decided Carol, pushing food listlessly about on her plate.

After Frank had gulped down his last cup of coffee, he scraped back his chair with a muttered "S'cuse me," and stood up. "Guess we'd better be gittin' back to them sick cows of ours, Mr. Boyd," he urged.

Her father put down his napkin at once and rose with a hasty nod.

"Sick cows?" inquired Hildegarde, as soon as the men had departed. She turned to Carol. "Let's go out to the cow barn and see how the poor beasts are."

The other stared at her. "You can't be serious, Hilda!"

"But I am," protested Hildegarde. "I like animals. In fact, I like anything that has to do with a farm. Granny has a farm, you know, and I mean to take an agricultural course at college so that I can run it for her someday. She's promised me the job."

"What a queer ambition," drawled Carol.

Mrs. Boyd intervened. "Not at all. I think it ought to be most interesting, Hildegarde. Now don't bother with the dishes, girls. Just run along! As soon as I put Timmy to bed for a nap—he's going to stay up late tonight for that church supper—I'll make another cake to take with me, and then clear away everything together."

Thus dismissed, the girls bundled themselves into warm

clothing, and Carol reluctantly accompanied her guest out of doors. Once arrived inside the big, clean stock barn, fragrant with its smell of fresh hay, she found herself oddly interested in watching men and beasts, however. Time flew, and it seemed impossible that the short wintry afternoon had vanished when Timmy was sent to call them all back to the house.

"That was fun!" cried Hildegarde, drawing a long breath of icy air into her lungs as they tramped across the frozen ground. "Frank is simply a wizard in veterinary work, isn't he?"

"Um, I s'pose so." Carol's tone was noncommittal. Yet it had been thrilling when one of the sick cows, down for hours, had staggered to her feet and Frank had pronounced all the others out of danger.

But later, at the supper held in the basement of the little country church, Carol kept gazing in puzzled wonder at Hildegarde. Was the latter really enjoying the hit-or-miss meal, consisting of great platters of sliced ham and mounds of crusty bread and homemade pickles, eaten to the accompaniment of guffaws of laughter of hearty-mannered country folk? Or was she merely giving a good imitation of polite enjoyment?

Then, after supper, Carol came upon her chum, Laura Bennett, and her guest talking animatedly together. Poor Laura looked hopelessly plain and fat beside Hildegarde, but neither girl seemed aware of any difference as they discussed amateur plays and puppet plays which both had directed, it appeared.

"Well, I've got to go back to the stage now." Laura glanced at the platform which had been curtained off at one end of the basement, and before which, when the board tables had been cleared away, long rows of chairs had been placed. Fond mothers and fathers were already taking their places in the chairs. "We're giving a fairy play, and that naughty little

Billy Larkin is sure to be up to some mischief if you don't watch him every moment."

The next instant there was a childish scream from behind the curtain. Loud and frantic, it rose above the clamor of voices and laughter. "Laura! Laura, come quick! Fire!"

Such genuine fright was in the shriek that those in the audience who had seated themselves started to their feet. Laura turned and dashed for the platform, and Carol felt herself thrown roughly aside by someone's swift passing, saw Hildegarde stagger as she, too, was shoved against the wall in the wild stampede which followed.

As in a nightmare, Carol's feet seemed to become leaden, too heavy to move. She could only stand and stare helplessly at the curtained platform, perceiving with horror that the curtain was already blazing.

A woman's voice rang out. "We'll all be burned! This wooden building will burn like tinder. Let's get out! Let me out!"

And at once the stampede which had been headed toward the platform started back toward the narrow basement stairs. Shouts and screams filled the smoky air as the crowd surged in Carol's direction.

Then Frank leaped upon the platform, tore down the burning curtain, and stamped out the flames. He shouted, "Fire's out! Sit down, everybody. Show's startin'! Sit down!"

There was a tense, perceptibly questioning halt in the onrush toward the stairs until someone laughed hysterically. "Well, I sure thought we was all goners!" Then people began to drift back to their seats, shamefaced, calling children to their sides. And the scare was over.

Carol felt her hand clutched. It was Hildegarde. "Look!"

Carol saw her mother come across the platform carrying a small blanketed figure in her arms, and followed by another woman, weeping. She saw Frank stop her mother, speak to her, and an instant later, take the little figure into his own arms and step carefully down from the platform, while Mrs. Boyd tenderly wrapped in coat and shawl the sobbing woman who had followed her. Then Frank and the weeping woman came toward the girls.

"What'll I do, Frank, with her papa away and me alone on the farm?" whimpered the woman.

Frank's steady gaze was upon the stairs as he threaded his way through the crowd. He walked strongly, purposefully, speaking to the woman. "Little Peggy ain't burned bad. Don't you worry none, for it was mostly her cheesecloth wings what caught on fire. But, just for certain, we'll run her over to Doc Bowen's and let him look her over. You dressed warm enough, Mrs. Merrill? It's commencin' to snow out."

Then, when he had disappeared up the stairs, followed by Mrs. Merrill, there was a loud chord on the piano and there was Laura, playing the opening song of the fairy play.

Later, after festivities were over and everyone was preparing to go home, Laura found time to whisper to Carol and Hildegarde that little Billy Larkin had caused the trouble by striking matches—"for fireflies," he said. But he had been well spanked by his father. "I'll bet he won't try any more firefly tricks." Laura chuckled. "By the way, Carol, your mother has asked me to dinner tomorrow. It may be a blizzard that's coming across the prairies, but it'll take more than a blizzard to keep me away."

Sure enough, although snow was drifting high across meadows and roads the next day, Laura arrived, red-cheeked and breathless, at noon. "Oh, *yum*—roast chicken, hot biscuits, and chocolate cake! I can smell 'em all!" she cried ecstatically as soon as she entered the living room. She found Carol and

Hildegarde setting a temporary table Mr. Boyd had established in there. "And dinner out of the kitchen!" finished Laura.

"Isn't this fun?" exclaimed Hildegarde. "Mrs. Boyd is going to let Carol and me serve and not get up once from the table! She's going to be a lady of leisure!"

"Good! What shall I do?" Laura popped out into the hall, divested herself of heavy outdoor apparel, and was back almost at once.

"Take Timmy out from under our feet!" chorused the other girls. So, with a laugh, Laura enticed the youngster over into a corner to amuse him.

More than once, during the dinner that followed, Carol looked around the table. Her mother had dressed with care in one of her "good" gowns left over from better days, the girl noted, and she looked like her old self. As for her father, his sensitive, scholarly face was alive with mirth as he teased the girls and carved second and third helpings. Timmy was too hungrily consuming his dinner to be more than a picture of a small boy eating chicken, and Frank was the same as usual, except that he wore his Sunday suit—an atrocity in blue-green woolen with a bright crimson necktie. But somehow today, remembering Frank's air of authority when he had reassured the sobbing mother about her child's safety, Carol realized that he did not seem merely a "hired man."

Why, he's a fine person, thought the girl, amazed. He's the sort of man people respect. There's a word for what he has to offer others—what is it? "Mother," she asked aloud, "what's the word that means being so honest no one ever doubts you?"

"Integrity?" supplied Mrs. Boyd, smiling.

"That's it!" Carol looked down at her plate of chicken and creamed onions and fluffy mashed potatoes and cranberry sauce. Her thoughts went on shaping themselves into silent sentences. Frank has integrity—and when a man has that he has about everything worthwhile, even if he does use bad grammar and wears a red necktie with a green suit! Come to think about it, that's what folks around here all have—integrity! That's what makes our country so great, because integrity goes with love of freedom and respect for others' rights.

"A penny?" Hildegarde's laughing voice startled Carol from her reverie.

She shrugged. "Not worth even that, I'm afraid."

Dishes were done in rapid time, with Mrs. Boyd under strict orders to stay out of the kitchen. Then, through the dark, snowy afternoon, the girls made fudge, laughed together, and had fun as only girls can when there is a feeling of storm outside and cozy warmth within walls.

At dusk the telephone rang and Laura, summoned to it, returned with a sparkling face. "Mother wants to know if I may stay all night?" she cried. "The blizzard's getting worse."

"Why, of course." Mrs. Boyd nodded. She went on thoughtfully, "Poor Mrs. Merrill, all alone there on her farm! I wonder how little Peggy is tonight?"

"Lots better," grunted Frank, from the chair where he had been dozing. "In fact, she ain't hardly burned a mite. She was around playin' with her dolls today."

Everyone but Mr. Boyd stared at him. "Why, how do you know?" asked Carol.

Mr. Boyd laughed. "You forget the Merrill youngster is a sort of patient of Frank's. He took his old car and drove over six miles, through the blizzard, to find out how she was today. Tough going, though, wasn't it, Frank?"

"Yeah," answered Frank. "Kind of. Had to walk the last two miles. The car got stuck in a drift." He yawned.

"How'd you happen to go?" asked Carol. "The doctor said she was all right, didn't he?"

Frank glanced at her. "Well, I sort of figgered out, what

with Peggy's dad bein' away, her mother'd feel better if she had one of the neighbors droppin' in." Yawning again, he rose and stretched. "Guess I'll turn in. Good night, everybody."

"Don't you want any supper?" demanded Timmy.

"Supper? After all I et this noon! You'd better not eat too much supper, neither, young man, or you'll be kioodlin' with one of them nightmares o' yours." Frank grinned down at the little boy.

"Well, I think we'd better all turn in," began Mr. Boyd. But at Timmy's roar of protest, he stopped to chuckle.

Later, after sandwiches and milk and the remains of the cake, the three girls made their way upstairs. It was even colder than usual, going through the tiny front hall, for an icy wind, borne upon the blizzard, seemed to sweep beneath the door, rattling windows, where Mrs. Boyd had previously made up a bed for Laura upon the couch. But once the bedroom door was closed against draughts, the place grew cozy and warm from a stovepipe which rose from the living room below.

The girls sat brushing their hair before they got into bed. Carol began to giggle at the sight of Laura wrapped in her mother's old bathrobe. "I declare, Laura, you're so hefty you look more like you ought to be my mother than Mother does herself."

"Fifty-one, fifty-two," Laura stopped counting strokes of her hairbrush, to give her good-natured laugh. "Now that's something to live up to," she said comfortably. "Even being mentioned in the same breath with your mother is a compliment."

Hildegarde's brush also paused. "Listen! I hear singing. Is it your mother, Carol?"

"Yes, Timmy must have had one of his nightmares after all, and Mother is singing him back to sleep. Why?" inquired Carol.

"She has a marvelous voice," breathed her friend.

"She graduated from the Boston Conservatory. Didn't you know she used to be soloist in a church there before we had to come to Iowa?" said Carol.

"And she gave up her position to come out here to do farm work because your father decided on the Midwest?" Hildegarde put down her hairbrush and hopped into bed.

"Of course." Carol nodded. Then she laughed. "Mother couldn't bring the position with her, could she?"

Hildegarde did not laugh, however. Instead she said slowly, "Carol, you're certainly lucky, with parents like yours! There is your mother, pretty, talented, out here doing ten servants' work because she thinks it's her job. There's your dad, starting all over again! But it's your mother I'm thinking about. Why, do you know she hasn't stopped working since I came, nor stopped smiling except when she was taking care of little Peggy Merrill? She's tops, if you ask me!"

Laura jumped beneath the blankets on the old couch. "You bet she's tops!"

Carol stared at them. Then tears stung her eyelids, and she bent and blew out the oil lamp. What a blind, selfish little fool she had been! She had been ashamed of her mother! My goodness, she wasn't fit to tie her mother's shoestrings, and she had been ashamed of her!

Slowly she groped her way over to the bed she was to share with Hildegarde and climbed into it. As soon as she lay down, she felt her friend's arms around her, giving her an affectionate hug.

"You're not bad yourself," said Hildegarde sleepily. "You're a lot like your mother, Carol."

"Oh, no, I'm not!" gulped the other. "But—but I'm going to try to be!"

"That's the proper spirit," called Laura from the couch.

Then she added threateningly. "Now you two be quiet, or I'll come over and get in between you, and then where'll you be?"

"On the floor!" groaned Hildegarde. "There's not room for three of us in this bed, when one of us is Laura!"

After the laughter had subsided, Carol lay quiet. It was nice to feel Hildegarde's friendly arms around her, even when those arms relaxed in sleep. Nice to hear, presently, the soft, regular breathing which came from Laura's corner. She lay listening to the howling of the blizzard outside and imagined it sweeping across the open prairie land. It seemed impossible that the land had ever been hot, and heavy with corn, and that, instead of the shrieking of the wind, summer nights had been loud with insect music. She thought of Frank, tramping through the blizzard just to bring the comfort of a friendly face to a lonely farm woman. She thought of her father, fighting month in, month out, against odds of financial worry and lack of agricultural knowledge, to make a living and a home for them, her mother and Timmy and herself. She thought of her mother, whose unfaltering devotion was the cornerstone upon which that home was built. Oh, never again would she question such devotion! Instead, she'd do her part to help.

Carol sighed with contentment before finally drifting off to sleep, for the last thing she heard was her mother's voice, singing Timmy's lullaby. Voice, lullaby, blizzard wind mingled together and became one, blending at last into a prairie song of striving and courage, of life and love.

# Journey to Elkton

CONSTANCE PULTZ

# Journey to Elkton

Whose idea was it? Not one could say. There was just the conviction that Life, in passing, had paused to administer a peremptory tap on the shoulder.

"What," it had wanted to know, "are you waiting for? Time is fleeting!"

And, clearly, by that was meant the fact of Ernie's being nineteen and Christina just past seventeen. Life had implied that it didn't intend to stand around cooling its heels forever, and so the idea had had to be born.

Now, on the first Friday of November, all the plans were laid. Christina's bag was packed, as was Ernie's, and Fred and Lisbeth had dressed themselves circumspectly in the gray tweed suits that made them look more than ever what they were—a pair of red-headed, tilt-nosed twins with a gay brain apiece and a disdain for the commonplace. As circumspectly as they dressed, Fred and Lisbeth would dine at home this Friday evening, as would Ernie with his people and Christina with hers. Eight-five or eight-ten would find Fred and Lisbeth strolling over to Clinton Street with the newest Cozy Cole

215

records, there to join Christina in seeing her parents off to a bridge-and-late-supper. Ernie would happen by a trifle later, at the wheel of what had originally been his father's Pontiac, circa 1935. Once, therefore, the dissecting of Mr. Cole's recordings had been accomplished, it would seem only natural to measure the gas in the tank and then to tumble into the Pontiac and head for Mullins Hill to enjoy the weekend special of Dancing-and-All-the-Cokes-You-Can-Drink-for-Fifty-Cents. This was a routine to be veered from only inasmuch as they did not take the road that lurched northwest to Mullins Hill, but the one that turned southeast across the state line into Maryland.

Ernie said they couldn't hope to make very good time. "On account of the tires, you know. Plus the general state of her very wobbly insides."

Christina smothered a meaningless giggle. Her wrists felt curiously cold, her face hot. She tried to explain this by declaring aloud, "I knew I should have worn my lambskin," as if this trembling inner excitement could be molded and quieted by the mere weight of a winter coat.

In the back seat Fred and Lisbeth were squabbling cheerfully over a bag of peanuts that Lisbeth had succeeded in dragging up from the depths of Fred's pocket. How could they chomp away at nuts at a time like this? Christina refused their offer of a share with what she intended as a gaily brittle commentary: "I took an oath last year never to eat peanuts on my wedding day."

Once the words were out, of course, she wished them back. They sounded hard, rather than brittle, and certainly not at all gay. She stole a glance at Ernie to see if he had noticed, but he looked precisely as he had looked the last time she sought visual contact with him. His eyes were fixed on the road, and his hands concerned themselves with a steering wheel that boasted cousinly connections with a shell-shocked broncho.

Christina thought, There are at least twelve girls in school who'd give half their hair to be where I am right now. And that in itself was a spine-jelling realization. The cold in her wrists increased, her heart beat very fast, and she tried to remember how all this between herself and Ernie had started. It seemed like yesterday, or a week ago Tuesday, or only the minute before last. And yet it was six months to a day since the spring dance when, at three-quarters of an hour past nine, she had left off swinging her French compact by its silver chain and talking eighteen to the dozen with Lisbeth to respond to the age-old "Mind if we dance this one?"

That had constituted the lifting of the curtain on Ernie Dole, with a wrestler's chest and a runner's legs and a smile that left Van Johnson with a long way to go. One dance with Ernie had multiplied to a total of five or six, one Saturday night grew to a dozen such Saturday nights, with hikes and Sunday suppers and stage shows at the Palace thrown in for good measure. The first kiss had led to a swapping of rings, and both had led to this—a night ride to a town where marriage was easier than in any other, and where no one inquired too closely into the matter of birth certificates.

"Golly!" whispered Christina to herself, and swallowed a shiver, and rested her shoulder against Ernie's arm, and said again, "Golly!"

"Doing pretty well for an old wagon like this." Ernie made the announcement in a voice that was the echo of her own emotions. She saw him mentally exploring his pockets to make certain he had the ring.

In the back seat Fred was assuring Lisbeth that he had not forgotten the rice. "It's stowed away, safe enough. Plenty for us both."

Lisbeth remarked pensively that she couldn't think back to when they'd had the chance to throw a bit of rice. "Matter of fact, I can't remember when there's been an elopement of any kind. Not since we were twelve, I'll bet, and then it was only Aunt Portia, who was fifty if she was a day. Positively, she must've found it chilling to think of everybody standing around in church and staring at what she'd hooked after all these years. Remember how she said to Mr. Peebles, 'Honey, let's slip off to the Poconos instead,' and they did, and never came back for a year, and by that time everybody had forgotten why they went away?"

Lisbeth sighed zestfully, cracked another peanut shell, and flipped it so that it sailed across the the front seat and landed like a finishing touch to Christina's hairdo. "I love weddings," she said. "I must have one of my own someday."

There wasn't much traffic on the highway. Ernie said something to this effect, clearing his throat in order to do so, and Christina, also clearing her throat, said rather senselessly that she supposed it was because of the weekend coming up. No one added anything to that, and for a while Christina tried to count the number of telephone poles they passed. But her mind kept switching back to the contents of a note she had left propped on her mother's dressing table.

"Don't worry," the note had said. "I'm quite safe. Ernie and I are getting married, and please don't feel it's something that shouldn't be. We are going to be very, very happy." She had added two postscripts. One said, "Back on Monday," and the other, "I love you both very much." It seemed, on reflection, a feeble parcel of words to cover a matter of such moment.

At exactly eight-forty-nine they passed through a town called Rising Sun, and Fred made a crack about "Old Sol so solly, but he in process of setting over Japanese Empire . . ."

At eight-fifty-nine the right front tire collapsed, slowly but definitely, like a balloon with an invisible leak. It didn't seem practical to fumble with a flat in what Lisbeth called the dark of the moon, so they bumped on for another quarter mile to something known as Squeak's Filling Station, Repair Shop, and Eat Bar, and there sat around a catchup-spotted table and drank Cokes while Squeak wrestled with the remainder of the right front tire.

Christina decided that Squeak's place had character, but lacked charm. A green and greasy lamp swung over the cash register, and a couple of ancient calendars decorated the wall. All about there was the smell of mustard and soft drinks and crankcase oil, lightened by a minor cadence of hamburger. Christina sniffed and sipped. Now and again Ernie's knee touched hers, or she and Lisbeth accidentally scuffed each other's toes. What sounded like a heartbeat was in reality the uneasy ticking of a footless clock that shared a shelf with salt-cellars and vinegar cruets. Christina looked around at every-one and smiled—rather gallantly, she supposed.

"Look," she cried, "shouldn't we drink a toast? Isn't that the accepted thing—a toast to the bride and groom?" The words scratched her throat in the saying, and so she repeated them firmly. "Ladies and gentlemen—the bride and groom!"

She and Ernie and Lisbeth and Fred stood and solemnly clicked bottles. A trickle of sweet stuff slipped down four throats simultaneously. Then Ernie was laughing and pushing her into her seat.

"You don't drink to yourself! You never do that."

So he and Christina sat, fingers entwined, while Fred and Lisbeth swallowed and toasted for a second time. It was all very fine and very right.

Squeak came in wiping the grease from his hands onto his

pants, saying the job was done. "Should last you another fifty —seventy-five miles, that tire. Careful driving, that is."

While Ernie dickered over the bill—"Manlike," whispered Lisbeth to Christina—Fred approached one of the calendars and with a pencil drew a heart and the names "Ernie Dole" and "Christina Martin" and the month and the year.

"Romantic!" said Fred, chuckling, and he reached in his pocket to sprinkle a little rice on the floor of Squeak's place for, as he said, luck.

Sweet to the nostrils, chilly to the flesh: that was the night air and Christina was glad enough to take refuge in the car and wait while Squeak pulled a rag from somewhere and gave a polish to the windshield.

"Going to Gretna Green?" he asked, and there might have been a hint of wistfulness in his voice. Glancing at his face, Christina discovered that, underneath the oil smudges, he probably wasn't much older than Ernie and Fred. "I've been there in my time," he said, and all at once he seemed as ancient as the phrase sounded ominous. "Quite a little town it is. They fix you up in short order, too. See this?" Christina caught the gleam of a wedding band. "I still wear it. For a laugh now and then."

Christina huddled more warmly into her coat and wished they were off and away. She resented the fact that Squeak had not confined himself to windshield-wiping and a discussion of the bill. She wanted to prod Ernie and cry, "Come on, what are we waiting for? It's getting late."

"I was only a kid," said Squeak with a last flick of his rag, "when I got married. Nineteen. She was younger than that. The whole thing was over in a week, annulment and all. It was a funny thing . . ."

And even when they'd left Squeak behind and were once more panting along the highway, Christina felt five words buzzing like gnats in her ear. Squeak had said, "It was a funny thing."

There was nothing much about Elkton to take the eye. Christina told herself that she'd expected more than this—prim streets, prissy little houses with square lawns, and flower beds gone dry with cold. Only the signs on the lawns were worth a second glance. There were quantities of these, each a duplicate of all the others. "*Justice of the Peace*," they said, and there was something Big Town in the fact that often the words stood out in electric lights. Ernie brought the car to a halt at the corner of a street whose name Christina could never afterward remember, and they all got out and went up the walk of one of the prissy little houses with its Big Town sign.

"This looks all right," said Ernie, elaborately offhand, and Christina, not to be outdone, agreed enthusiastically that it did and that she didn't know when she'd seen a cuter-looking house.

Mounting the steps, Fred and Lisbeth began to hum a scrap from *Lohengrin*. "Dum-*dum*-de-dum, Dum-*dum*-de-dum, Dum-*dum*-de-dum—" they sang, with appropriate glances at Ernie and Christina.

Fred punched the doorbell, and while they waited he pretended to perk his tie and set straight the shoulders of his coat.

"Have to look properly dignified," he explained to Ernie. "Your hair's a bit unsettled. Better whip a comb through it."

Absently, Ernie passed his palm over his crew cut. It seemed to Christina that he jumped visibly when the door opened and a pint-sized creature peered skeptically at them from behind a curtain of bangs.

"You want the Doctor?" she asked, and Fred, experimenting with humor, assured her that they were in the market for marriage, not an appendectomy.

The pint-sized creature countered with a withering frown, then mustered them down a six-foot hall and shut them into a room of potted rubber plants and peeling leather chairs that smelled rifely and lemonishly of furniture polish. Footsteps roamed overhead, as though in perpetual search of something, and a radio drummed jazz in a distant region of the house. Ernie cleared his throat and looked at nothing. No one spoke. No one sat down. It occurred, irritably, to Christina that they must resemble a cluster of political prisoners on point of trial. To offset this, she brought out her compact and powdered her nose, ostentatiously inspected an eyebrow and surveyed a fading freckle. The palms of her hands were moist and, covertly, she wiped them with her handkerchief and was glad to hear footsteps descend the stairs and approach along the hall. She held her breath in the second before the door opened and Dr. Jones presented himself. He was wearing house slippers, a plaid sports jacket, and a pair of paint-smudged trousers. He carried a rather clinical-looking black book, and his jaw chomped rhythmically over the remains of what was presumably a pre-bedtime snack.

He smiled rubberily, pairing Fred with Christina and Ernie with Lisbeth, and exclaimed, "A double ceremony? Ah, two sets of happy children!"

Gently, Fred set him right. "Just a single today, Dr. Jones. The rest of us are witnesses."

"Ah?" The word came gloomily, some of the rubber left Dr. Jones's smile, and it was with an air of condescension that he arranged Ernie and Christina in the proper positions, flanked by two of the peeling leather chairs and with the odor of furniture polish stronger than ever where they now stood.

Fred and Lisbeth, it was plain to see, were in their element.

They stood smartly at attention, tweed shoulders touching, eyes suspiciously lively under innocent lids. In an indigenous Fred-and-Lisbeth sort of way, they looked very charming.

This is a big day for them, thought Christina. And the phrase caught her up sharply. It was odd to think of it as being Fred and Lisbeth's day. A little nervously, she succeeded in reminding herself, It's mine—my day. It belongs to me and to Ernie. It's ours.

She stirred her feet on the roses of the rug and wished somewhat desperately that Dr. Jones, as he opened his book, looked rather less like a bartender going over his accounts. She wished even more desperately that Ernie would bend his head to smile at her. He stood so close that if either of them had moved an inch their hands could not have missed meeting. But there was on his face the curious, locked-in expression that was blood-brother to her own.

Unctuously, Dr. Jones began to read, pausing now and again to suck a tooth or refocus his glasses. He dealt with customs and legalities, promises and devotion, with man and woman and city and state, and particularly he dealt with those now gathered together in his presence and desirous of entering into the exalted companionship of matrimony. Whether his words were those of the prescribed ceremony, or whether they were the outward form of an inward imagination, no one of his audience was prepared to say.

Something in Christina nudged her. It's queer. Like getting married in a play.

She wiped her palms and stole a look at Ernie, who had chosen the same moment to steal a look at her. Perspiration beaded his lip, and there was the possibility that he would look like this if he were in the act of wrenching his ankle. And she remembered, with something of a shock, that she had never seen him wrench an ankle, or cut a finger, or even break a nail. She had no idea how he behaved with a cold in the head, or how he reacted to badly-brewed coffee. In his turn, he didn't dream how dreadful she could and did look in curlers, or how addicted she was to reading poetry aloud every night before falling asleep, and practicing French verbs early Sunday morning in the shower. What, too, if they didn't agree about the right and the wrong man in the next election? Christina bit her lip. How silly of us, she mourned, not to have talked just a little bit about such things.

Admittedly, Ernie looked divine on a tennis court, danced a fine conga, and swam like a fish. He adored her, just as admittedly, and that, of course, was important. But he adored her right now, as of this minute, and there were a number of things about herself at this minute that she was preparing to change in the next two or three years. What if he didn't admire the changes?

Swallowing, she began slowly to back across the room. "I'm sorry . . ." Could that be her voice, pinched, like a finger in a too-tight ring? "I'm sorry, but—oh, *golly*, Ernie!"

She thought she would weep; but suddenly there was no need for that. Ernie had whirled and was catching hold of her hand and holding it in the warmest of his grips. His voice, too, sounded pinched. "I know. I know how you feel. Don't be sorry. Please don't be sorry."

It happened like that, abruptly, briefly, and was summed up more or less adequately by the pint-sized creature as she showed them from the house.

"I knew the minute I looked at you that the ceremony wouldn't take!"

And she slammed the door on their heels, presumably in an attempt to draw some of the sting from a wholly personal insult.

There was a fresh, new smell about everything on the drive

home. A page might have been turned in a book, or a furrow in a field. Nobody said very much, for there was still the slight conviction of foolishness that comes when one has, at the last moment, swerved from the accomplishment of a plan that had seemed so wonderful at its inception.

Only the twins, so unfeelingly deprived of their lark, sulked in the back seat and cracked peanut shells and flipped them into the curls atop Christina's head.

"I," Lisbeth could be heard to mutter with what she undoubtedly hoped was true sarcasm, "must have a wedding of my own someday."

Christina and Ernie smiled at each other, and Christina huddled pleasurably against the increasing cold and thought, Someday we'll have a real wedding, with a church and a minister.

Recalling "Dr." Jones and his plaid sports coat and rubbery smile, she gave an involuntary shudder. Everybody will be there, she told herself, planning this marriage of a not-too-distant future. Lisbeth can wear a floppy hat and dance with all the ushers, and Fred will be near enough the age of discretion to be trusted with the ring.

Aloud, she said thoughtfully to Ernie, "I didn't think very much of that town, did you? That—Gretna Green? That Elkton?"